The Most Beautiful Woman

in Spain

and Other Stories

Domingos Monteiro

Translated from the Portuguese
by Alison Aiken

CENTER FOR PORTUGUESE STUDIES
UNIVERSITY OF CALIFORNIA, SANTA BARBARA

EDITOR
João Camilo dos Santos

ASSISTANTS TO THE EDITOR
Eduardo Viana da Silva
Rodrigo Bauler
Megan Turner

DESIGN
Sasha "Birdie" Newborn

Contents

The Most Beautiful Woman in Spain   5

A Tale to the Contentment of All   17

The Hungarian Teacher   43

Sleep   60

Purity   72

The Day of Reckoning   90

Revenge   100

The Most Beautiful Woman in Spain

'Foreign?'

The man had been standing near my table for some time, but I had pretended not to notice him.

'Yes.'

'Portuguese?'

'Yes...'

'Well I'm Spanish.'

'I can see.'

I couldn't have been more offhand. This rude interruption had disturbed my thoughts. Sitting on the terrace of a café in the Plaza Mayor, I was entranced as I studied the elegant ornamentation in the square while at the same time, in an idle historic digression, I was trying to identify the coats of arms of the kings above the porticos. It was a hot night and Salamanca smelled sweetly of a mixture of hay and cut wheat which came from the plateau and combined with the subtle perfume of the past that emanated from the centuries-old façades of the buildings like a distant memory.

I had arrived in Salamanca from Paris that afternoon and was on my way back to Portugal and, as I usually did, had decided to stay for a few days in the city which, since my first visit, had been for me a living piece of history, art and culture. As I watched the noisy crowds in the square go by I relished my solitude, a solitude that can only be truly enjoyed when one is unknown and surrounded by other people. However, the man speaking to me was not one of those who hold back.

'D. Ramiro Soares,' he introduced himself. 'D. Ramiro Soares, tourist guide. At your service. And you are...?'

I had to give him my name.

'May I?' And without waiting for assent he pulled a chair and sat down.

I began to feel very annoyed and asked angrily, 'What kind of tourist guide? What's there to see in Salamanca at this time of night?' And I looked meaningfully at my watch, which showed past midnight.

'Everything, sir.'

'Every what? The university is closed. The cathedral is closed...'

D. Ramiro didn't give a direct reply and remarked, 'The university is magnificent, isn't it? Have you seen the miraculous stone, sir? The stone that fell on to the labourer and didn't crush him?'

'Of course I've seen it.'

'Ah, but what you don't know is that the man was my grandfather.'

'Your grandfather? Are you sure?' My surprise was genuine and my incredulity justified. I repeated my question, 'Are you sure?'

'Absolutely, sir. My grandfather used to talk about it a lot, and his greatest delight was to show the scar. People used to come from all over Spain to see it. There was even someone who offered him a 'duro' to touch it. But my grandfather was very conventional and wouldn't allow it.'

I was immensely amused and disputed this sardonically.

'Don't forget that the New Cathedral was built in the sixteenth century.'

'Well, yes – in the sixteenth century,' D. Ramiro admitted without looking at all embarrassed. But that's of no account, sir. My grandfather was very old.'

I looked at him carefully for the first time. He was tall, slim, had thin lips and a pointed chin, with a thick moustache and large, dark, lively eyes. He must have been older than fifty and was dressed strangely: a braided jacket, a stiff collar and gold buttons, no tie and a grey, broad-brimmed hat. There was something of the toreador about him and of D. Quixote, or at least of the sort of person we Portuguese think of as being like D. Quixote.

Realising he was being studied, the man assumed the air of someone who is about to be painted and smiled a smile that was both proud and welcoming.

'D. Ramiro,' I said to him, for the first time calling him by his name, 'would you like a drink?'

The man didn't wait for me to press him and without allowing me to insist, called out, 'Pepe, bring me an anis.'

The waiter obviously knew him well as he asked, 'A double, D. Ramiro?'

'Of course, a double.'

The ice between us had broken and I began to feel warmly towards him. D. Ramiro swallowed his medicine in one gulp and stood up.

'Right, let's go,' he said decisively.

'But there's nothing to see, D. Ramiro,' I countered hesitantly.

'Nothing to see? That's the best I've heard in all my life. There's everything, sir. Everything that can only be seen at night.'

The insinuation was obvious, though I pretended not to understand.

'The monuments are closed,' he admitted disdainfully. 'How old are you, sir?'

'Twenty-seven.'

'Twenty-seven? So why are you concerned about the monuments? The tombs are closed as well, but that certainly isn't bothering you. However, the streets aren't closed.' He pointed up to the sky. 'And the moon isn't closed either. Life, sir, doesn't close at the same time as the cathedrals. Come on!' he continued authoritatively.

I paid the bill and got up obediently.

We crossed the brightly-lit square. D. Ramiro walked in front waving his arms and making remarks that I found hard to understand. Besides which I wasn't paying much attention. I could see that D. Ramiro talked for the sake of talking. We went down some almost deserted, dimly-lit streets which, with the full moon shining on the ancient buildings, had an unreal softness.

I was relishing the enchantment of the night and, indifferent to the loud pronouncements of my companion, was studying in the silence the shadow of a past which was in part robbed of its dignity and mystery by electricity and daylight. I felt grateful to D. Ramiro. This Salamanca, which I thought I knew so well, was for me entirely unknown and I wouldn't have minded spending the whole night wandering along its twisting streets breathing in the learned, medieval perfume that emanated from them. The mysterious voice of poetry awoke in me and I

7

began silently to recite the verses which Antonio Machado had written about Soria:

¡Soria fria! la campana
de la Audiencia dá la una.
Soria, ciudad castellana
¡tan bella! bajo la luna...

and I applied these words to Salamanca.

'Here we are, sir.'

D. Ramiro's loud voice pulled me back into the present.

'Here where?'

'The first station in our excursion,' and he cheerfully imitated the sound of a train's whistle.

From half-open folding doors came the sound of a guitar and the noise of stamping flamenco dancers. We went in.

It was a modest provincial show put on for students. D. Ramiro chose a table and, entirely at ease, ordered, 'Joselito, two anis. A double for me. A single for the gentleman.'

'No, a vermouth for me.'

D. Ramiro repeated, 'A vermouth for the gentleman and a double anis for me.'

A dancer was twisting her body on a small stage to the sound of the guitar. She was a very ordinary dancer, lacking soul, for whom the 'olés' from the audience induced no enthusiasm.

I lowered my eyes with the sense of sadness and embarrassment that I feel whenever I go to a badly-performed show.

D. Ramiro understood and asked, 'Don't you like Spanish dance?'

'I do like it, but it's got to be good.'

'You're right. She's lousy. Joselito!' he called out. 'The bill,' and he added scornfully, 'Where did you manage to dig up that dancer?'

'What's wrong with the dancer, D. Ramiro?' the waiter asked insolently.

'What's wrong, man?' He pursed his lips angrily and said imperiously, 'She should be shot.'

'Not quite that,' I murmured, trying to keep the peace.

I paid and we left.

There was no music or dancing in the first house we went to. A group of cheerful girls were laughing loudly. D. Ramiro was welcomed effusively.

'How good to see you, D. Ramiro. Viva, D. Ramiro! We thought you must be dead!'

'Dead? Me?' and he went on, 'I'm immortal.'

They had surrounded him, squealing, and one of them asked, 'What have you brought us today, D. Ramiro?'

D. Ramiro assumed a mysterious air and discreetly pointing to me declared solemnly, 'A prince.'

'Bravo! Bravíssimo!' they screamed in unison.

D. Ramiro made a gesture as though dispersing a swarm of annoying flies, 'A prince, but he's not for any of you. Where's Conchita?'

'She's sleeping,' one of the girls told him. And she went on sarcastically, 'She's always sleeping.'

'Well, yes,' D. Ramiro acknowledged, 'but she's worth more than all of you put together. Go and call her and bring us something to drink. The usual. Yes, the usual. No, not for the gentleman – bring him a vermouth.'

He turned to me and whispered, 'Now you're going to see a real woman.'

'Let the poor thing go on sleeping,' I balked. 'Another time...'

'Sleeping? She's not one to sleep. She's got fire in her veins. You wait and see.'

When Conchita entered, rubbing her eyes, as though trying to put him right, D. Ramiro said, 'Conchita, look what your fame's brought you – His Highness has come from Paris just to see you. Look after him well.' Then he walked purposefully away.

'From Paris? Pleased to meet you,' she said, starting up the conversation.

'It's a pleasure, Conchita,' I replied politely.

'It's beautiful, Paris, isn't it?'

'Very beautiful. Don't you want to sit down?'

We sat at a distant table and Conchita asked, 'French?'

'No, Portuguese. And I'm not a prince.'

'I know. I know D. Ramiro.' Then with a practised movement she stroked me and, using 'tu' as she spoke to me, asked, 'Don't you want to come with me?'

'Not today.'

'Don't you fancy me?'

I looked at her carefully. She was quite a young girl, but her youth was already withered by the onslaughts of mercenary love.

'I fancy you a lot. But I only arrived today and I'm tired.'

'I'm very tired too,' she confessed. 'Yesterday I had quite a time here.' Then she added with a degree of pride, 'Lots of people ask for me. D'you know what I mean?'

'I do,' I said, forcing myself to be diplomatic. 'We'll make it another day.' And I put a note in her hand. 'Drink my vermouth.'

The girl drank it, clicking her tongue, then thanked me.

'Thank you. You'll come back tomorrow, won't you?'

'I'll be back,' I said, without conviction.

We had said all we were able to say to each other and neither of us believed the promise.

In a corner of the room D. Ramiro was telling a story while one of the girls sat on his lap. The others stood round him, laughing loudly.

'D. Ramiro is worth his weight!'

'And you weigh more than you're worth!'

Seeing me standing beside him, D. Ramiro stood up. 'Already?' he asked, surprised. Then he turned to Conchita and admonished her, 'What did you do to the gentleman?'

'Nothing,' I intervened. 'It's entirely my fault.'

Once in the street I expressed the desire to go back to my hotel, but D. Ramiro stood in front of me, his arms outstretched, and declared, 'Sir, don't disappoint me so! For twenty years I've been showing visitors the nocturnal delights of Salamanca and not one of them could ever say that I – that I, D. Ramiro Soares, Castilian and gentleman, disappointed them.'

The anis was beginning to show its effects and his eloquence was rapidly gaining momentum. 'I can see that you are demanding. So am I. But however demanding you are, you won't be disappointed. So far we haven't got beyond the aperitif, just the aperitif. We haven't got to the *pièce de résistance* yet, and that's something not a single man can refuse. I sympathise with you,' he went on protectively, 'and I'm going to show you something I've never shown anyone.' He emphasised the word, '*Anyone.*' 'It's the most rare, the most precious thing you could imagine. But if I'm going to reveal the secret to you I need you to,' and he went on solemnly, 'to swear that you'll never tell anyone. Not anyone, *not even in Portugal.*'

The fatigue and tedium that were beginning to assault me disappeared and, fascinated and amused, I agreed, 'I swear, D. Ramiro.'

'Very well. Come with me.'

We went along more streets and arrived at a small square. D. Ramiro stopped suddenly again. 'Here,' he said, as he held out his arm and showed me the door to a house, lowering his voice, 'is the home of the widow of a Spanish grandee. She's very proper and everyone, even the neighbours, think that she leads an impeccable life. However, as her confidant, I know a man – a banker from Madrid – who comes to visit her secretly once a fortnight. This is the woman I'm going to introduce to you, not because she's the widow of a *fidalgo* and the lover of a banker, but because as far as I'm concerned, she's worth more than all the monuments in Salamanca and is, without doubt, the most beautiful woman in Spain!' In a voice vibrating with lyrical enthusiasm that I believed to be sincere he went on, 'I, D. Ramiro Soares, am going to have the honour of showing a foreigner, a lover of beauty, the most beautiful woman in Spain! One moment, sir.' And he expounded grandly, 'I shall see whether it would please her to receive us.'

I stood where I was and D. Ramiro nimbly crossed the square and knocked on a door. Some minutes later a peephole in the door was opened and a head appeared. From where I was I could see him gesticulating and hear the strident sound of his voice. It was after two in the morning. The woman must have been in bed and there was some unforeseen problem. D. Ramiro's eloquence – and I knew it from experience – was, however, insuperable and, after a long dialogue, he signalled to me.

I approached. However, the door didn't open at once and I felt I was the subject of minute examination from the other side of the peephole, through which the light of an oil lamp was projected. My face can't have been displeasing since, after a few moments, a husky voice murmured, 'Come in, gentlemen.'

We went up the stairs behind the maid – an angular old woman with the air of a guardian of clandestine love affairs – and once in the sitting room, after putting down the lamp and inviting us to sit down, she told us, 'Madam is just coming.'

Ten minutes later *the most beautiful woman in Spain*, as D. Ramiro had called her, stood portrayed in the doorway. If I hadn't already been prepared for her I should have been disappointed. She was a tall woman who, in her time, must have been beautiful. Now, around forty years old, her beauty had almost completely disappeared in

11

the increasing plumpness which disguised the elegance of her figure and gave her face that particular appearance of a woman who puts on weight as she reaches a critical age. However, her flowing hair and large black eyes retained the freshness and brilliance of her youth.

We stood up. Solemnly, D. Ramiro made the introductions.

'Doña Pepa, D. Domingo, my close friend.'

'How do you do.'

'How do you do. Please sit down.'

We sat and Doña Pepa laughingly chastised him, wagging a finger at him. 'You made a lot of noise at the door, D. Ramiro. You know I don't like that.'

I could see that she was a woman of standing whom the misfortunes of life had brought down but who wanted to retain the appearance of dignity and who was still jealous of her reputation which – contrary to what D. Ramiro stated – must have been quite shaken.

'Please forgive me, Doña Pepa.'

'This time you're forgiven.' And turning to me she asked graciously, 'What would you like to drink?'

'Nothing for me, Doña Pepa, thank you.'

'As you wish. As for D. Ramiro, I already know what he likes.'

She stood up and called from the door, 'Dolores, bring D. Ramiro's anis.'

When the maid entered, carrying a glass and a full bottle of anis on a silver tray, D. Ramiro's eyes lit up.

'Doña Pepa,' he said, 'would you like to show my friend your collection of paintings?' And turning to me he added, lying quite naturally, 'It's the collection I told you about, the one that's got a Velazquez.'

'I've already told you it's not a Velazquez,' Doña Pepa said to him. 'It's a Ribeira. And there are even doubts as to whether it's that.'

'All the same to me,' said D. Ramiro placatingly.

I liked this way of keeping up appearances and I found the story of the collection a delightful euphemism.

'It's very late, D. Ramiro,'

'Late? It's never too late to see something beautiful, D. Domingo. You're not going to waste a unique chance in your life,' he said, irritated.

'Wouldn't you like to see my collection?' Doña Pepa asked, her eyes pleading.

'With great pleasure, Doña Pepa.'

I stood up and went with her into the inner part of the house.

§

When we returned to the sitting room some time later the bottle of anis was empty and D. Ramiro was humming.

'Darling,' Doña Pepa murmured affectionately in my ear, 'D. Ramiro is an excellent man, but he's very drunk. You're going to have to take him home.'

'Is it very far?' I enquired.

'No, about three hundred metres. At the end of the first street, on the right, number eighty-four.'

D. Ramiro was miming as though playing a guitar. From his mouth came guttural sounds which he believed were a *canto hondo*. He hadn't yet noticed us. I shook him and jokingly reprimanded him.

'D. Ramiro, Castilian and gentleman, let's go.'

D. Ramiro tried to get up, to no avail.

'Let's go, D. Ramiro,' and I helped him to stand up.

'So how was it?' asked D. Ramiro like someone coming out of a fog, then seeing a sign from Doña Pepa, he went on, 'What did you think of Doña Pepa's collection?'

'The best I've ever seen.'

'Thank you,' and she kissed me maternally on the forehead.

We took our leave.

'Till tomorrow, Pepa.'

'Till never again, darling,' she murmured, gently melancholic.

The door was shut and the chill air of the dawn struck our faces. D. Ramiro seemed to be himself again. His legs were giving way, but his tongue was once again loosened.

'A good woman,' he said, referring to Doña Pepa. 'But she's a wreck now.'

'A wreck, "the most beautiful woman in Spain"?'

D. Ramiro clung more firmly to my arm and repeated, 'The most beautiful woman in Spain. Who told you that lie?'

'You did.'

'Me?'

He let go of my arm and took a few hesitating steps but his legs

13

wouldn't hold him up and he clung onto me again.

'D. Domingo,' he said solemnly, 'I love you like a son.'

'Thank you, D. Ramiro.'

I tried to get him to move but he fought me off, resisting obstinately.

'D. Domingo, I've got a confession to make to you.'

'Keep it for tomorrow, D. Ramiro.'

'No, it's got to be today, D. Domingo. I'm a fake. I'm the biggest fake in Salamanca.'

'Maybe you're not, D. Ramiro.'

'I am, I tell you I am. Don't tell me I'm not, D. Domingo. I'm a liar, an incorrigible liar.' He became more and more agitated and it was only with all my strength that I managed to make him take some steps. 'But now,' he went on, 'even though it hurts me — and only God knows how it hurts me! — I'm going to tell you the whole truth. My grandfather,' and here he lowered his voice and spoke confidentially, 'had already left this life for a better one when I was born. As far as I know he didn't have a scar, and he didn't have a stone hit him on the head.'

'What a pity, D. Ramiro!'

'Of course, it's a pity, D. Domingo, because it always brought me in a bit of cash.'

I went on pulling him, but D. Ramiro was obstinate.

'D. Ramiro, it's time to go home.'

'Go home? Me? Without keeping my promise? No, D. Domingo. Let you go home and say that I, D. Ramiro Soares, didn't keep my word? Never! No, I'm not going home without introducing you to "the most beautiful woman in Spain". It's near here, D. Domingo,' he pleaded. 'This time I'll get it right – it's just a short walk.'

'No, D. Ramiro. Leave it for another day.'

D. Ramiro could hardly stand on his legs but with the stubbornness of drunks he continued to resist. I put my arm round his waist and, with an enormous effort, crossed the square and took him down the road.

When we arrived at the door of the house, D. Ramiro, who was completely intoxicated, clung to me, crying.

'You're a bully, D. Domingo! And me, D. Ramiro Soares, I'm a man without honour.'

I knocked at the door. After a long delay a figure appeared at the window.

'Who is it?'

'It's me,' yelled D. Ramiro, 'me, a man who can't keep his word.'

'And don't I know it!' At which a torrent of bitter, marital abuse in Spanish spewed from the open skylight.

Then the voice suddenly fell silent and another figure appeared.

'Forgive me, sir. Just a minute. I'll come and help you.'

'No, you don't need to.'

The door opened and I dragged D. Ramiro along as best I could. The stairs were steep and when I arrived at the top my heart was beating rapidly.

'Thank you, sir. Come in. Rest a bit.'

Exhausted, I accepted the invitation and fell into a chair. I let my eyes travel round: it was a modest, clean sitting room. At one end there was a shrine with an image of the Virgin and a votive lamp. D. Ramiro, who was muttering meaningless words and continuing to say he wasn't a man of his word, was taken by someone into the house.

I got up to leave and raised my eyes. In front of me was a tall girl wrapped in a cotton dressing gown.

'Thank you so much, sir. Thank you so much. I'm embarrassed for my father.'

'It really doesn't matter, señorita.' And I asked, 'Señorita...?'

'Guadalupe. Maria de Guadalupe.'

'Señorita Maria de Guadalupe,' and I fell silent, embarrassed. I couldn't take my eyes off her. Her black hair was in braids, she had a clear, oval face and enormous brown eyes that were infinitely gentle. Her slim, well-shaped body was like the trunk of a young palm tree. Everything that the sun and the charm of Spain have to give to beauty was there in front of me.

'Señorita Maria de Guadalupe,' I said, taking out a fifty-peseta note, 'please give this to your father.'

She refused, but I insisted, 'Give it to him, and tell him from me that I, D. Domingo, solemnly declare that he, D. Ramiro Soares, even though he is unaware of it, kept his word. Goodbye, Señorita Maria de Guadalupe.'

'Goodbye, sir. Thank you.'

I went down the stairs and wandered aimlessly.

When I came to myself I realised I was leaning over the bridge.

The Tormes, made shallow by the August heat, ran between the pillars. And I, absorbed and enraptured, could see reflected in the fleeting water the image that I had seen only once but which would remain fixed in my soul for ever – that of the most beautiful woman in Spain.

A Tale to the Contentment of All

Quando mermó su riqueza,
era su monomanía
pensar que pensar debía
en asentar la cabeza

Y asentóla
de una manera española
que fué casarse con una
doncella de gran fortuna;

Campos de Castilla, António Machado

I

D. Ramón de Torrelavega y Iglesias del Madrigal de las Torres Altas got out of the armchair in which he had been sitting, blew his nose loudly and going to the window called out in a loud voice:

'Pedro!'

There was no reply and D. Ramón repeated the call still more loudly:

'Pedro!'

The courtyard remained deserted. Some hungry hens were searching for food in the cracks between the stones, a dog was curled up sleeping beside a bench and in the golden, calm morning D. Ramón's voice went on calling in vain, thundering through the air, insistent and useless. With an angry gesture D. Ramón closed the window and returned to his chair. He remained still for a few minutes with his eyes closed. A deep vertical furrow ran down the centre of his brow. D. Ramón was thinking. In the four decades of his life this had occurred only half a dozen times, not because he was stupid but because the activity of thinking when not directly related to a clear, concrete fact, appalled him as though a heresy. Thinking was, for him, the occupation of priests and doctors, anyone who had to be concerned with other lives, not something for someone who, as he had always done, wanted to live his own life, intensely and fully.

That morning, however, the phenomenon occurred and D. Ramón was astonished to discover himself starting to find enjoyment, though bitter enjoyment, in his disturbing interior wandering. It is true that something had happened that had caused this: D. Ramón had celebrated his fortieth birthday the previous day and had lost 100 duros at poker, a debt which he had to repay by six that evening (D. Ramón honoured his gaming debts, indeed these were the only debts he honoured) and he had the vague realization that he was ruined. He still had doubts as to this, though, and it was only Pedro, his steward and agent, who could explain things to him. For years D. Ramón had signed cheques and documents without caring about reading their content, with the same lack of interest and supreme indifference that a head of state signs laws and decrees that he is enforcing. Pedro kept the accounts; Pedro acted as his proxy on his many and frequent legal papers; Pedro did the buying and selling: Pedro was the one who knew. But where was Pedro?

Suddenly he recalled the subtle warning from Carolina, his housekeeper, who was away for a few days visiting her family and who had pronounced with that shrewd, sharp distrust women have, 'Why don't you take a look at Pedro's accounts, D. Ramón?'

'What for? To find out whether he's robbed me?'

'I don't want to say exactly that, D. Ramón. But everyone should take care of what belongs to him,' she replied evasively.

'Carolina!' D. Ramón had said seriously, 'for three hundred years the Torrelavegas have been robbed by their agents. And I'm not going to be the last representative of such a glorious line and end such an honourable tradition.'

'D. Ramón, you know...' and she had remained looking at him with that look that is at the same time gentle and angry with which mothers look at their sons who, because of their age and position, are beyond the reach of a parent's reprehension and punishment.

D. Ramón had forgotten Carolina's words, just as he forgot everything that didn't interest him much, but now they were coming back
to him with uncomfortable insistence. D. Ramón got up anxiously and
went to lean against the balcony window that looked onto the property.

D. Ramón's house was built on a small hill overlooking a plateau.
It was the end of April and fields of wheat and verdant rye stretched
as far as the eye could see. A light breeze made them billow, giving
the fleeting impression that an invisible hand was stroking the moving
waves. It was like an ocean held down by its roots where, from time to
time, harsh silhouettes of oak trees rose up like small boats with grey
sails.

A dusty road cut across the plateau from one side to the other and,
in the distance, far away at the ends of the horizon, the hills of Ávila
rose in a blue mass, an uprising of the earth. Half a league away, form-
ing a brown, stony island with its manor houses, its interior courtyards,
its narrow road and church towers, Peñaranda de Bracamonte lay idly
beside the road.

The morning was slipping by and D. Ramón continued to stand
still against the window's railings. A vague dreaming had followed his
interior, real and insistent meditation and, after being immersed for a
long time in the blue sky, where a stork was gliding, his eyes travelled
distractedly above Peñarenda. They rested on the verdant wheat fields,
drawn hypnotically by the force of the fields' germination, whose constant, disturbing mystery escaped him entirely.

Part of the land belonged to him, but D. Ramón no longer knew
what were its boundaries, because of all the sales, mortgages and prom-
issory notes into which he had indirectly entered.

A feeling of remorse and a bitter sense of betrayal of the land
overcame him suddenly and D. Ramón closed his eyes, covering them
entirely with his flattened hand as though wanting to hide from himself
an offence and a crime for which he was responsible.

The fields were his, but up to what extent they were his only Pedro
could tell. And where was Pedro?

As though in order to reply to his silent question, a figure mounted
on a bay horse appeared at the end of the road that led to the entrance.

'Pedro,' D. Ramón bellowed angrily from the window as the man

19

arrived in the courtyard with its flower beds in front of the house, 'since when have the stewards of the Torrelavegas been absent without the permission of their masters?'

'You know, sir,' Pedro replied without any embarrassment as he dismounted, 'that it's since the seventeenth century, as you can discover in the library archives. But this time that wasn't the case. I did no more than obey your orders, sir.'

'My orders? So what orders did I give you? What did you go and do?'

'Sell the pair of oxen at Peñaranda market.'

'The pair of oxen? Which pair?'

'The only ones we had.'

'The only ones? Are you telling me, useless man, that I told you to sell our only pair of oxen?'

'Not exactly. You didn't tell me to sell anything. You were a bit...' he hesitated a moment searching for the right word, 'a bit out of it, you called me in a loud voice and said, "Pedro, I've got a debt of honour to pay before six in the evening tomorrow. I need a hundred duros." And as I argued, quite truthfully and politely, that you hadn't got the money, you told me, "Well go and fix it." "How?" I dared to ask. "The how is up to you", you replied. "Get it somehow. If you don't produce it tomorrow I'll tear out your beard." So for love of my beard, which by the way I don't have, I decided to carry out your orders and sell the pair of oxen.'

He stopped talking and calmly began to tie the horse's reins to a ring on the wall.

D. Ramón found this amusing and roared with laughter.

'Come on up. We need to talk.' And he closed the window.

Two minutes later Pedro entered the room. He was a short, fat man with thin lips and black eyes that were small and thoughtful, betraying intelligence. Above his high forehead, which was lengthened by the beginnings of baldness, was a black lock of brilliantined hair pulled forward, displaying a preoccupation with elegance which his smooth face and white, manicured hands confirmed. He was wearing town clothes, a jacket, trousers, highly-polished shoes and a brightly-coloured tie. With a briefcase under his arm, at first sight he looked like a notary's assistant coming to draw up a deed.

'At your service, sir.'

As they stood facing each other one could not imagine two more dissimilar people, although they were more or less the same age.

Unlike Pedro, D. Ramón was tall and thin, with large bright eyes and thick, blond hair that was swept back. He was carelessly dressed – a hunting shirt, breeches and high boots and only his well-cut moustache, a narrow line shadowing his upper lip, demonstrated an interest in his appearance.

Different though they were, inside and out, there was however something that made them similar and this, perhaps the result of their long-standing relationship, was probably the irony, thoughtful in the one, while superficial and flippant in the other, with which the two observed life's problems.

'Sit down.'

Pedro remained standing.

'Sit, I told you. We've got to talk seriously.'

Pedro sat down and D. Ramón then sat facing him across the other chair, his arms leaning on its back.

'Pedro,' he said in the tone of one waiting for an unnecessary acknowledgement, 'what's the state of our finances?'

'Our finances, D. Ramón? Your finances, is that what you mean?'

'You've always confused the two, Pedro. Far too much. Why separate them now?'

'Time and your comments have cured me of that bad habit,' Pedro replied in the same tone.

'That's a bad omen, but whatever you say. So, what's the state of my finances?'

Pedro hesitated a moment and then replied evasively.

'Confused... Very confused, D. Ramón.'

'I hate confusion,' D. Ramón objected vigorously. 'Let's get down to solid facts.'

'So where would you like me to start?'

' "Oraiendus ab initio" as Ulpiano said,' replied D. Ramón, who pretended that he had studied Law in Salamanca twenty years earlier.

It was the only Latin phrase he knew, but he liked to use it.

' "Ordiendus" as who used to say? I don't understand, sir.'

'Of course you don't understand. For all your pride you're nothing more than a complete ignoramus. It means, "Let's start from the beginning"'

'And what's the beginning, D. Ramón?'

This time it was D. Ramón who hesitated.

'The beginning? The beginning? The banks, for instance. What deposits have we got, or rather (as you must have much more), what deposits have I got in the banks?'

Pedro opened the briefcase and took out a small oilskin-covered book which he began to leaf through slowly. Then, having got to a particular page, he put on some tortoiseshell-rimmed spectacles and asked with a businesslike voice, 'Would you like to sit down, sir?'

'Not necessary. I can do the sums in my head and shouldn't get too tired.'

'Right. In the Bank of Bilbao you have the princely sum of two pesetas forty. In the Bank of Estremadura, three pesetas fifty. In the Bank of Spain... let's have a look.' He removed his spectacles, wiped them carefully, put them back on and remained silent, his eyes fixed attentively on the bottom of the page.

'Well?' D. Ramón pressed him ironically. 'Is the sum so astronomical? What the hell are you thinking about?'

'I'm thinking, D. Ramón... I'm thinking that you have the honour of having the smallest deposit there is in the Bank of Spain: two cents precisely.'

'Two cents?' D. Ramón laughed. 'Two pretty pennies? Well that's really original – something that could only happen to a Torrelavega...'

'In the Bank of Andalucia...'

Pedro went on with his reading, but D. Ramón interrupted him.

'That's enough, Pedro. I'm in the picture. If you know the total, tell me.'

'Well yes, I know it, D. Ramón.' He turned the page and read in a solemn voice, 'Twelve duros and seventy cents.'

'Twelve duros and seventy cents? Well you can't say it's a fantastic amount. But it doesn't matter.' Then he went on pompously, 'Now you should know, Pedro, that a Castilian nobleman might love gaming, wine, bullfights and beautiful women. But never money. Love of money is for merchants and Jews.' His voice became grave and deep. 'A Castilian nobleman can also love the land. And I...' he hesitated, as though finding it hard to make a confession, 'And I, contrary to what you might suppose, love the land.'

He stood up, opened the window and, making a sweeping gesture that encompassed the entire landscape he asked, 'And all that? What is there of all that?'

Pedro had also stood up and remained silent. D. Ramón closed the window again and leaning there in front of Pedro, commanded him, 'I want to know everything, hear me? Everything.'

'Whatever you want, sir,' Pedro agreed, somewhat surprised by this serious behaviour.

D. Ramón pressed his eyes with two fingers like someone making an effort at deep, difficult reflection and then started to ask, 'The buildings in Peñaranda?'

'Sold.'

'The fields in Ribeira?'

'Mortgaged.'

'The estate in the Álamos?'

'Mortgaged.'

'The farm at Madrigal de las Torres Altas?'

'Also mortgaged.'

'So all in all,' D. Ramón concluded, a little anxiously, 'it's mortgaged in its entirety?'

'No, D. Ramón. The mansion and the estate around it aren't mortgaged.'

D. Ramón gave a sigh of pleasure and murmured with some relief, 'Well so much the better, Pedro... So much the better.'

'No, not so much the better, D. Ramón. So much the worse.'

'So much the worse? I don't understand.'

'I'll explain, D. Ramón... It's that there's a registered document acknowledging a debt; a debt that's larger than the value of the property.'

'So...' D. Ramón said after a minute's silence, then resuming his usual ironic tone he went on, 'so in your opinion I'm utterly ruined?'

'Utterly, D. Ramón,' Pedro confirmed without mincing his words.

'Pedro,' D. Ramón asked after walking round the room several times, 'how long do you think this can last?'

'Well, sir, until the creditors want...'

'And who are the creditors?'

'There are lots, D. Ramón. Though in actual fact it's only one – that is, only a woman.'

'Who?'

23

'I've already told you several times, but you never paid attention.'

'But who, man?' Ramón insisted impatiently.

'Ibañes's daughter.'

'And who is Ibañes?'

'Who was he, D. Ramón. He's dead. He was that man your father threw out from the assembly ball with his wife. His wife is dead too.'

'I do vaguely remember having heard about that...' D. Ramón muttered. 'But how is she the sole creditor?'

'Because she's buying up all your debts at the asking price and even paying more than their true value.'

'That's quite something!' D. Ramón remarked, surprised. 'And why is she doing that?'

'Through hatred, D. Ramón.'

'Through hatred?... Hatred of whom?'

'Of you, sir.'

'Of me? Why of me? I don't even know her... Explain.'

'It's easy, D. Ramón. Her father never forgave your father for the offence against him. Her father died and so did yours. And this woman, who seems smart, has decided to make use of her inheritance.'

'So it's hereditary hatred?'

'Exactly.'

D. Ramón's face lit up with satisfaction.

'Well that's something I admire and understand. Better due to hatred than sordid profit.'

'The result is the same,' Pedro reasoned.

'That's true.'

They fell silent. The morning was wearing on. A gust of heat that smelled of crops mixed with the scent of the earth entered the window. A light breeze rustled the leaves of the plane trees in the garden, a hen clucked in the courtyard and the entire room was suddenly filled with a hushed though insistent sound of germinating life.

D. Ramón breathed in the air deeply and the slight oppression that was beginning to overwhelm him disappeared completely.

'Pedro,' he said, cheerful as ever, 'what solution do you think there can be to my problem?'

Pedro was waiting for this question and for some time had been prepared for it. He belonged to a line of agents of the House of

Torrelavega and at some time or other the same question had been posed to each generation.

'D. Ramón,' he said gravely and respectfully, though with a slight flash of irony, 'in my humble opinion there are three solutions to the problem. But with due respect, they would all be very hard for you.'

'Maybe not, Pedro. Let's have the first.'

Pedro didn't reply directly and limited himself to asking, 'Have you read the letter from D. Juan de Torrelavega, your dead father's second brother?'

'From my uncle in Peru? The one in which he refuses the loan of 30,000 duros that I asked him for?'

'That's right. The one in which he says,' Pedro went on to quote, '"that he's not prepared to lend 30,000 duros (although he does have it) to be lost at gaming tables, in gambling houses or to be spent on imported French women..." But did you read it right through?'

'No; I only read up to there, and that was enough.'

'Well it's the end that's interesting. Do you want to see, sir?' And without waiting for a reply he took a yellowing piece of paper from his briefcase and read, ' "However, there is a house for you here, Ramón, a house for your use where you may carry on the activities of a man who is still young. If you decide to break with the family's tradition of idleness, as I did, then all you have to do is cable me and I shall send you the money for the journey immediately.'

'So that's the first solution?'

'Precisely.'

'It's no good. On to the second.'

'Well it's also very difficult, knowing your character, D. Ramón and I don't know if I should...'

'Don't hold back... Get on with it.'

'Well, with great respect, it's the one adopted by your great-great-grandfather.'

'The one who shot himself in the chest with a rifle as he couldn't pay a gaming debt?'

Pedro nodded.

'That's no good either, although I don't think it's as bad as the first. Let's move on to the third.'

'The traditional solution?'

'Why traditional?'

'Because it's the one that's been adopted successively for the last three generations.'

'And what's that?'

'To marry well,' Pedro replied with laconic circumspection, and he went on, 'If you will allow me I'll explain.'

'I'm all ears.'

Pedro assumed the air of a professor about to give a history lecture and began, 'Your great-grandfather, the son of the one who killed himself, didn't have two pennies to rub together when he married Doña Pepa Ruiz, a rich noblewoman from the Estremadura. D. Rodrigo de Torrelavega, your dead grandfather, was completely ruined when he contracted a marriage with Doña Joana Iglesias, and your deceased father, D. Afonso de Torrelavega y Iglesias had everything mortgaged, just like you, when he was united in marriage with your illustrious, much-lamented mother, Doña Lucia de Madrigal de las Torres Altas.

'And I,' D. Ramón remarked, highly amused, 'whose full name is D. Ramón de Torrelavega y Iglesias del Madrigal de las Torres Altas, am to marry...'

'You,' Pedro cut him short with an air of importance, 'don't have much choice. Anyway...'

'Anyway,' D. Ramón challenged him.

'Anyway, D. Ramón, I have already drawn up a list...' And with a delicate movement he took from his waistcoat pocket a small piece of paper which he held out to D. Ramón. 'Would you like to take a look sir?'

'Well, of course,' said D. Ramón grabbing the paper. 'You really are a thoughtful man.'

He looked at the list for some time, firstly with amused interest and then with a furrowed brow.

'Pedro,' he asked, scowling, 'this Doña Matilde de Peñaranda, isn't she the one with a squint?'

Pedro confirmed this with a slight movement of the head.

'And Doña Lucia Muñoz, isn't she a widow?'

'Yes, sir, she is.'

'And Rosa Alvarez? How old is Rosa Alvarez?'

'D. Ramón,' Pedro replied, taking offence at the caustic irony in which the questions were being posed, 'I'm well brought up, and I've never asked her age.'

'Fine, Pedro. That's a good enough answer. In that case I know that Doña Rosa has already reached the stage when it would be impolite for a man to ask her age. Shall we put it at fifty-five, do you think?'

'Perhaps...'

D. Ramón crumpled the paper and hit the table.

'So we're saying that in Peñaranda and the surrounding area there's not a single woman, young and without physical defects, who could marry me?'

'There are some, D. Ramón. It's just...'

'It's just?'

'It's just that they're not rich.'

'Well that's no good, Pedro,' D. Ramón agreed firmly, 'because I, D. Ramón de Torrelavega y Iglesias del Madrigal de las Torres Altas, however penniless I am, will only marry a young, healthy, woman who's not secondhand... And who's rich, of course.'

'As you wish. I wash my hands of it.' And with a respectful weariness he went on, 'You don't need me for anything else? May I go?'

'You may.' And he thanked him cheerfully. 'Thank you. You did what you could.'

'Don't mention it, D. Ramón.'

He rose and went towards the door and was about to go through it when D. Ramón called him back.

'Pedro!'

'D. Ramón?'

'You're so stupid. You forgot one.'

'Who, D. Ramón?'

'Ibañes's daughter.'

'Soledad Ibañes?' he asked, astonished. 'She would be the last one I'd think of, D. Ramón.'

D. Ramón didn't pay any attention to this and asked, 'Do you know her?'

'I know her by sight.'

'And what's she like?'

'Very beautiful.'

'And young?'

'She can't be thirty.'

'Single?'

'I assume she is. Yes, she's definitely single.'

'Come here, Pedro, and look at me.'

Pedro went up to him and D. Ramón put his hand on his shoulders and, standing over him at his full height, continued, stressing his words, 'Well then, Pedro, it's Soledad Ibañes's hand that I'm going to ask for. That's if I like her, of course.'

'Sir,' Pedro remarked, looking at him as one looks at a man who is not right in the head, 'Do what you want, sir... If it were up to me, I'd prefer to strut up to a bull unprotected, like the bullfighters do in Portugal; and a bull with its horns without any covering, at that...'

II

'No sooner said than done' was D. Ramón's motto.

The following day, immediately after lunch, he called Pedro and told him to bring the carriage round.

'To go to Peñaranda?' Pedro asked, still hoping that his master had abandoned the previous night's decision.

'To go to see Doña Soledad Ibañes.'

'Would you allow me, sir,' Pedro broke in, his reasoning rising against what he classified as total madness, 'with all due respect to give you my modest opinion?'

'As you wish, but if it's in order to dissuade me, I'll tell you right now that there's no point.'

'All the same, D. Ramón, my conscience as a faithful servant obliges me to do so.'

'Well then, be brief.'

'Have you thought of the consequences that may arise from such an ill-considered act? If, as everything leads one to believe, you are not received, or if you are received, but in response to your request you are given a peremptory and unpleasant 'no', have you thought what it would mean for the honour and tradition of this house?'

'That's enough!' D. Ramón interrupted. 'I've already thought of all that, and I have to tell you that I've been thinking more in the last two days than I have done in my whole life. My decision is final.'

'D. Ramón!' Pedro begged, pleading.

'I've already said, that's enough!'

Confronted with such an imperious attitude from his master, Pedro went to prepare the carriage and at three o'clock precisely D. Ramón, in formal dress, quietly climbed into the ancient vehicle.

However, before D. Ramón arrives at the house of Doña Soledad Ibañes, the author must make something clear to his esteemed readers. Given that D. Ramón's decision is final, and since the author has promised in the title that he will write a story to the contentment of all, he feels obliged to point out, before events take their inevitable course, that, apart from what actually took place, this story might have had two alternative endings: either D. Ramón, spurned and utterly ruined, shoots himself in the head, following the miserable example of his great-great-grandfather – a most agreeable solution for those many persons who enjoy unhappy, or dramatic endings; or, having decided against making a plea at the last minute, he resolves to accept his uncle D. Juan's invitation, thus giving testament to his subjection to the respectable principle of elevation in status through work, a solution to which, for obvious reasons, D. Ramón has, up to this point, shown himself thoroughly opposed. This last solution should give moral satisfaction to those who believe (and they know why!) that 'idleness is the mother of all evils.' Those of my readers who are demanding, given the above, may choose either one of the two and bring the story to an end. However, if your curiosity is stronger than your hopes and convictions, which is almost always the case, then you will see that Fate, even when it has a literary character, respects neither the intentions of the author nor the wishes of his readers. So it was that, when the author created an idle, gaming D. Ramón who is impulsive and proud and has a concept of honour peculiar to himself, and a rich and beautiful Doña Soledad who, besides this, possesses a lively and impetuous character, he could not fail to allow them the freedom to continue according to their nature and to be subject to all outcomes, given that he believes in the real lives of his characters. For this reason, as you will see, the story ends up having a very different ending, but the author retains the hope that it will still be to the contentment of all.

D. Ramón's house was a league from that of Doña Soledad. It was a hot afternoon and during the journey, in spite of Pedro's efforts, D. Ramón remained silent and inscrutable. It was only when they arrived at the small park of Judas trees, firs and camellias that surrounded the fortified house, and precisely when the carriage stopped in front of the main entrance, with its drawbridge lying across a ditch full of honeysuckle and lilac, that D. Ramón pronounced his first words.

'Pedro,' he said laconically, 'go and deliver this note.'

Pedro took the letter with a trembling hand and, without daring to read it, went towards the door, where he knocked twice. A minute later a servant dressed in black livery arrived to open it. Confronted by such a person, Pedro recalled his position as butler in a noble house and, summoning his pride, commanded in a dry tone,

'Go and give this card to your mistress.' And he then added, 'From D. Ramón de Torrelavega y Iglesias del Madrigal de las Torres Altas.'

Doña Soledad was brushing her hair at the dressing table after her siesta when her nurse knocked on the door.

'Soledad,' the nurse said, 'a visitor for you.'

'For me? At this time of day?'

'Yes. An extraordinary visitor! You'll never guess.' And she held out the note.

Doña Soledad read out loud:

' "D. Ramón de Torrelavega y Iglesias del Madrigal de las Torres Altas requests of Doña Soledad Ibañes the honour that he be received on a private matter." Well, that's something! That really is something! Mónica,' she asked the nurse, 'what do you think the man wants of me?'

'Well what do you think he wants of you? Aren't you his only creditor?'

'But he doesn't know that.'

'He's obviously found out.'

'What's he come here for, Mónica?' she persisted.

'He's come to ask for a delay, or something like that. To ask for mercy.'

'Do you think so?'

'I'm absolutely certain.'

Mónica went to the window and lifted a corner of the silk curtain. D. Ramón had jumped down from the carriage and was standing waiting, his head raised. The sun was beating down on his fair hair and his tanned face.

'But I'll tell you one thing,' the nurse remarked, lifting her eyes, 'and that's that he's a good-looking man.'

'Oh, but you've recently begun to think that all men are handsome.'

'What do you want, child?' she agreed, smiling. 'I'm at an age when you can't be too demanding.'

Doña Soledad rose and went to have a look.

'Well,' she said, 'a man like many others. An ordinary man,' she asserted, lacking conviction.

'Are you going to receive him?' the nurse asked.

'What do you think?'

'Why do you want to know what I think? You always ask for my advice and then do exactly what comes into your head.'

'That's true. But tell me, all the same.'

The nurse hesitated.

'Look, I don't know if you want me to tell you. Perhaps it would be better not to receive him.'

'Well then, I'll receive him,' Doña Soledad responded promptly. 'I could say that I shan't receive him, but then I wouldn't know what he wants. So,' she went on, frowning, 'I'll work out how to humiliate him.'

'You never know with people like that,' the nurse interjected.

'Don't you worry about that.' And she went on, having made up her mind, 'Take him to the best drawing-room, offer him a chair and ask him kindly to wait a quarter of an hour.'

The nurse went out and Doña Soledad remained alone.

After a few moments she stood up, ran to the wardrobe and started to look for a dress. She took one, then another, and in less than a minute a dozen were spread out on the chairs, sofas and small tables in the room. Doña Soledad looked at them all, undecided, and after reflecting a while selected a black taffeta dress with no trimmings that was slightly low at the neck and tight round the bust, though it had a full, rounded skirt.

'A dress for solemn occasions,' she murmured to herself ironically.

Then, with meticulous care, she opened a drawer and took out a set of underwear. Finally she removed her silk dressing gown. Naked in front of the mirror she looked as though she had dipped herself in a lake of crystalline water. She shuddered slightly and for a moment remained contemplating, smiling at the woman with long, shapely legs, golden skin and small, firm breasts who was looking at her with her large green eyes, beneath the dark splendour of her black hair.

'Soledad,' she murmured, shaking a finger at the image, 'I don't trust you very much. Just look how you're behaving.'

And she began to dress with the precise movements of a person who is used to frequent changes of clothes. Once fully dressed, she went to look at herself in the dressing-table mirror and after touching up her hair, reddening her lips and putting two drops of scent behind her ears, she walked with determined steps towards the door.

When she went into the best drawing-room, D. Ramón, who was sitting, rose immediately.

'Sir,' said Doña Soledad, slightly bowing her head and without inviting him to sit down again, 'I have just received the most unexpected note that I have received in my whole life, and I confess that I haven't the least idea as to the nature of the private matter which D. Ramón de Torrelavega y Iglesias del Madrigal de las Torres Altas could have regarding Doña Soledad Ibañes.'

D. Ramón did not reply immediately. Never before had he seen such a beautiful woman, or so it seemed to him and, absorbed in this thought, he had completely forgotten the reason for his visit.

'Sir,' Doña Soledad remarked ironically, since the silence continued, and seeing herself being so foolishly and insistently stared at, 'my house is not exactly an art gallery.' And she went on drily, 'I'm waiting for your reply: what private matter has D. Ramón de Torrelavega y Iglesias del Madrigal de las Torres Altas regarding me?'

D. Ramón came to his senses. His mouth had become dry, just like when he was risking all his money on the final bet. It was with great difficulty that he managed to say,

'A thousand apologies, madam.' And giving into his impulsive character he went on, 'I had such a surprise that I was incapable of uttering a word.'

'Surprise? I don't believe that we know each other at all.'

'That's precisely why,' D. Ramón said, by now in control of himself. 'I was far from imagining that I should meet here, so close to me, the most beautiful woman I have ever seen.'

'And possibly the richest,' Doña Soledad added with meaning.

'That, madam, was only of importance up to the moment when I saw you,' D. Ramón asserted with total sincerity.

'Thank you for the compliment,' Doña Soledad said haughtily.

'However, I still don't know the reason for your visit.'

'Firstly, madam, as your neighbour, in order to present you with my compliments. I should have done so a long time ago, but I only learned of your presence here yesterday.'

'The courtesy of the Torrelavegas is in the blood – and well-known,' Doña Soledad said. 'And we, the Ibañes family, had proof of this not many years ago, when my father, Francisco Ibañes, and my mother, Dolores Ibañes, were compelled to leave the ball at the Assembly so that they would not sully the air that the noble D. Afonso de Torrelavega y Iglesias was breathing.'

'Madam,' said D. Ramón, who was not expecting such a direct riposte, 'I inherited from my father some possessions which I have squandered; I also inherited some of his qualities and some of his faults, but I did not inherit his hatred and ill-will.' And he went on, 'Nor am I responsible for his actions.'

'The noble D. Ramón de Torrelavega may give himself the luxury of pardoning offences which he has not suffered. The common Soledad Ibañes has no coats of arms other than the memory of the insults and stains that have blackened her red blood.' And she went on drily, 'Please continue.'

The conversation was starting badly, and anyone other than D. Ramón would have wisely and sensibly beaten a retreat. However, for D. Ramón, a fighting animal, Doña Soledad's words acted as an incentive and a spur. Besides this, Doña Soledad's repressed anger made her still more beautiful, and D. Ramón was extremely sensitive to beauty, even when, as in the present case, it assumed an air of rancour.

'Madam,' D. Ramón replied in a calm and decisive voice, 'before crossing the threshold of this house I had a specific plan: that of proposing to Doña Soledad Ibañes, my sole creditor, a conjugal union which would allow me to retain my property, while she would acquire the social position to which she surely aspires.' He paused and remained looking at the woman to whom he was speaking. Doña Soledad was expecting anything but this and she was so astonished that she was unable to say a word. 'Now, however,' he went on with composure, 'something so unforeseeable and strong has happened that I have to hesitate. That is…' He was silent again, still staring at Doña Soledad.

Doña Soledad didn't know whether to take D. Ramón's words as an insult or as an act of cynical frankness, and the most contradictory thoughts were going through her head. Among these, however, the greatest was a curiosity which she could not resist.

'And that is?' she asked, compelling herself to give her words an ironic, contemptuous tone.

'And that is...' D. Ramón said with conviction, 'something that would fast lead any other man to do the same...'

'What?' Doña Soledad asked.

'That I have fallen in love with Doña Soledad Ibañes. That I love you, madam.' And D. Ramón was utterly sincere as he said this.

On reaching this point the author finds himself obliged, much against his will, to intervene again in order to respond to the possible doubts of his readers who find it hard to believe that a man, most of all one like the hero of this story, could make the proposal he did, with such frankness, to a woman whom he has met for the first time. The author is also, of course, compelled to respond to the sceptical smile of those who doubt the sincerity of D. Ramón's sentiments.

To the former of these I would remind you of the many announcements in newspapers in which a 'respectable gentleman of about forty, of high social standing and a compromised fortune wishes to meet ladies under the age of thirty who are beautiful, rich and well-mannered'. These announcements are, usually, accepted quite naturally.

To the latter I shall simply say that – contrary to what they may believe – love, particularly in men, does not spring from knowing, but from not knowing, and from mystery and that the brusque, violent, almost instantaneous manner which was manifest in D. Ramón is in their nature, and rightly so (and this is what gives them their truly passionate soul).

With this in mind, let us see the reaction of Doña Soledad.

Doña Soledad quickly overcame her understandable surprise and did not wish to appear silenced by the daring and audacity of her interlocutor. She felt simultaneously flattered and offended, but leaving for later any analysis of the true nature of her feelings, what she wanted to do at that moment was to give him a lesson.

'Sir,' she said with haughty coldness, 'before his death my father charged me with dispossessing the Torrelavegas of all their possessions. The mission with which he charged me has been, one could say, fulfilled, and all that remains is to call on the law so that in a few months the last of the Torrelavegas is driven from his land. This obliges me, as an act of obedience to my father and in response to my primitive feelings, to refuse your proposal. However, something has occurred in my life which forces me to consider it somewhat less harshly. I am entirely indifferent to what you, D. Ramón, feel or do not feel about me, but the truth is that this may resolve a problem for which previously I could see no solution.'

She paused deliberately, a pause with her eyes constantly fixed on him in order to see his reaction, but D. Ramón's face remained inscrutable.

'What I am about to tell you, sir, is entirely confidential, although I am not,' and here she went on scornfully, 'going to demand of you a promise which I cannot be certain you will be able to keep.'

'Madam!' D. Ramón interrupted, his surprise now turning to anger.

Without taking note of the interruption, Doña Soledad went on, 'In a few months I am going to be a mother, the mother of the child of a man who, because of circumstances, cannot marry me. For me this is of no importance, since I am rich enough and independent enough not to be concerned as to what others think. However, I cannot say the same with regard to my child.'

She was silent again. D. Ramón was seized by increasing fury, a fury that stemmed not so much from the reaction to the insult represented by Doña Soledad's words but, strange as it may seem, from a form of jealousy felt by a betrayed lover. Neither the lack of reason for this, nor the lack of legitimacy, failed to lessen the violent, painful intensity. He wanted to scream out loud, voicing his internal revulsion, but something deeper, like a feeling of quiet dignity, forced him to remain silent.

'Sir,' Doña Soledad went on, coolly and solemnly, 'I accept your proposal on one condition. D. Ramón de Torrelavega y Iglesias del Madrigal de las Torres Altas will marry me and will retain his property. My child will be born legitimate. And I shall retain my freedom entirely,' she said, accentuating the words, 'including continuing to love the man I love.'

And since she felt that she had not spoken clearly enough, she went on to spell out her plan:

'And when my child inherits the property of the Torrelavegas

35

later, given the fact that obviously I shan't run the risk of having another child with you, D. Ramón, for my child would not be inheriting
anything more than that which already belonged to it and which, for
the moment, I temporarily hand over to you.'

She pulled the bell cord to call the servant. D. Ramón remained
silent in front of her.

'You have no need to reply at once,' she finished. 'All you need
do is send me a written response in the next twenty-four hours. Good
afternoon, sir.' And turning to the servant who had just entered, she
told him, 'Go with D. Ramón de Torrelavega y Iglesias del Madrigal
de las Torres Altas.'

'Good afternoon madam,' D. Ramón said, making a violent effort
to control himself. And turning his back on her, without another word
he left the room.

§

When Doña Soledad returned to her apartments, Mónica, who as
was her wont had been listening at the door and heard the entire
conversation, looked at her with a combination of admiration and
censure.

'Soledad! It's impossible! To talk about yourself like that!'

'It's of no importance, Mónica. Don't you think that a man who
sees me for the first time and has the audacity to ask me to marry him
and – what is worse – to say that he loves me, deserves a lesson? And
when you consider that he knows he's in my hands?'

'Maybe,' Mónica agreed, 'but you could just have rejected his
offer.'

'That wouldn't have been enough.'

'And what if he goes spreading about what you said?' Mónica
asked, putting in words what she mentally feared.

'He won't,' Soledad replied with conviction. 'And if he does, he'd
look ridiculous.'

'And if,' Mónica went on, 'he were to continue with his request in
spite of what you told him?'

'I don't believe he would. But if he does, then so much the worse
for him. I'll know how to get rid of him.' And she went on, changing the
tone of her voice, 'If you had seen how pale he turned, you would be

thinking he was even more handsome!'

Soledad's face became dreamy.

'Soledad,' Mónica warned her mischievously, 'don't go cutting off your nose to spite your face!'

'Good God, Mónica! Do you really think that a man – oh, and a woman too – could fall in love so quickly?'

'It doesn't often happen,' the nurse replied pithily, 'but it has happened.'

At which point the conversation came to an end.

As for Pedro, when D. Ramón reached the carriage, although he was seized with curiosity, he dared not ask a thing. He knew his master's quick temper and it was enough for him to see from his face that the interview had not gone as he had wished.

'Get down!' D. Ramón ordered Pedro, who was sitting in the coachman's seat. 'I'll drive.'

Contrary to his usual behaviour he whipped the horse and, with a jerk, the carriage departed at full speed. The wheels sparked in the gravel and the hedges and cornfields that lay to each side of the road swayed wildly. Pedro was sitting in the carriage, his heart beating rapidly, and when the carriage reached the entrance to the house a quarter of an hour later he found himself commenting, 'Oof, D. Ramón. I thought my last day had come.'

D. Ramón took no notice of this confession and drily ordered him, 'Upstairs.'

When they reached the drawing room, D. Ramón put a hand on his shoulder and speaking in a voice he had to force to be calm, asked, 'Do you think my uncle D. Juan might keep his promise?'

'Tell me, D. Ramón...,' Pedro began, anxious to get the confirmation of something he had already guessed.

'Give me the answer instead of asking questions,' D. Ramón interrupted coldly. 'And tell me what you really think.'

'Well, judging by what my father used to say, I think he would. Everyone who knew him said he was a man of his word.'

'Give me some paper for a telegram and a letter, Pedro,' D. Ramón said decisively. 'Paper engraved with the coat of arms.'

D. Ramón quickly wrote out the telegram.

'Take this to Peñaranda and see it gets sent off today.'

Pedro took the piece of paper and read in silence. The telegram simply said, 'I accept your offer and await your orders. Ramón.'

When Pedro got to the door D. Ramón called him back.

'How long do you think it will take for a reply?'

'I don't really know, D. Ramón. But judging by how long letters take I imagine no more than a month and a half or two months.'

'Fine. Off you go.'

D. Ramón was alone. His earlier anger was followed by a profound sadness, although it was not the result of the decision he had taken nor of the idea that he was about to lose his property and would have to leave his homeland. Nor again was it the result of the insult he had suffered. D. Ramón was a just man and he felt that, to a certain extent, he had deserved it. Besides which, naïve like all men, even the most experienced, he truly believed Doña Soledad's confession. And this is what hurt. In an unthinking moment, D. Ramón had confessed to being in love but now, after suffering such disappointment, he realised that he was, indeed, in love. This realisation came to him precisely at the moment when an unassailable wall had come between him and the object of his love.

D. Ramón grabbed a sheet of paper and began to write. However, five minutes later he crumpled up the paper and threw it on the floor. For an hour D. Ramón wrote notes and screwed them up. Finally, having decided upon the final version, he quickly wrote the letter, put it in an envelope and sealed it with the seal of his arms.

When Pedro arrived, D. Ramón simply said to him, 'Take this letter first thing tomorrow morning to Doña Soledad's house. There's no reply.'

§

Doña Soledad was still in bed when she received the letter. An inexplicable agitation prevented her from opening it immediately. It was an absurd feeling of fear, like the ones she felt as a child when going into a dark room.

'Mónica,' she asked the nurse, who was looking at her with amusement, 'what do you think he'll say?'

'I don't know. The best thing is to open it and find out.' And she went on sharply, 'By the way, there's no reply.'

Doña Soledad opened the letter, her hand shaking.

As she read it the worried expression on her face began to change. 'It's a refusal, Mónica, a refusal!' she shouted, absurdly happy. And she went on to read the letter out loud.

Madam

I am withdrawing my request. It cannot be hard for D. Soledad Ibañes, and you can count on my absolute discretion – to find someone who will grant you the service you desire, and for a lesser price than that which you would have to pay were it granted by me. It will also not be necessary for you to apply to the law in order to receive repayment of my debts. In exactly sixty days, Doña Soledad Ibañes, if it is your wish, you may send your agent to my house for the document to be drawn up detailing the handing over of all my property. Thus, as is your wish, you will be granted all the possessions of the Torrelavegas, less one which is, by its very nature, inalienable and is not in the form of money – their honour.

Ramón de la Torrelavega y Iglesias del Madrigal
de las Torres Altas

'There! He believed it!' she said jubilantly.

'Men are all fools!' Mónica declared, so stating a great truth. And she went on, 'What I don't understand is how happy you are!

'You don't understand?' And Doña Soledad's face took on an expression that was at the same time assured and smiling. 'It's that if he had accepted I should have been greatly disappointed.'

III

A month and a half later, just as Pedro had suggested, the reply came from D. Juan. D. Juan was generous beyond what had been expected. He sent a cheque for 30,000 duros payable by the Bank of Spain and allowed D. Ramón the freedom of choice as to whether to leave his homeland or not.

I have not forgotten – he wrote in the letter which accompanied the cheque – *that you are the only son of my eldest brother whom, in spite of the many differences there were between us, I esteemed and respected. You are, by traditional right, the head of our house and it is not for me to give you orders. I have had information from over there and I know that your property is tied up. If this money – which is all I can give you for the moment – can save you, then so be it. If not, and if it is your wish, come over without any fear or sadness, since this country, while being free and independent, is still Spanish territory.*

At any other time D. Ramón would have paid some of his more demanding creditors and lost the rest at the gaming table. However, he had made a decision and his state of mind – black depression which was not in keeping with his character – left him no other choice. He therefore sent Pedro to Bilbao to buy his ticket and kept the money that remained to be given back to his uncle.

The ship was due to leave three days after the day for the notarised document to be drawn up and D. Ramón was waiting impatiently for the moment when he could put the protective and consoling vastness of the sea between himself and that woman. He had had no news of her and vaguely knew, without having asked anyone about it, that she had gone to Madrid. In the depths of his conscience there was a hope of something he was unable to identify, but he dispelled it as though it were shameful. D. Ramón was still in love, and it was the worst kind of love – that love which, because it is ignoble, no man can confess to, even to himself.

It was the end of June and D. Ramón took long horse rides in order to while away the time. The wheat and hay had ripened and were being harvested and the landscape was beginning to appear much like the state of his mind. The plateau was once again to taking on a burned appearance, which is its mark and its emblem, and the horizon was losing the clarity of its lines in the rarefied air, being imprecise and indeterminate.

On the day that had been arranged for the deed to be drawn up the notary arrived at the arranged time together with witnesses. A quarter of an hour later, however, Doña Soledad's agent still had not arrived.

'Pedro,' D. Ramón asked impatiently, 'Did you tell him? Did you give him the time?'

'I did, D. Ramón, and I'm amazed. But he shouldn't be too long,' Pedro replied, going up to the window.

The atmosphere was heavy and D. Ramón was upset, in spite of his irrevocable decision. He had got everything prepared in order to leave immediately after the deed was completed, but it was only at that moment that he realized that what he was about to do was irrevocable and that leaving for ever the house that had been in his family for three hundred years was the end of a tradition and a lineage.

'A coach is arriving,' Pedro said suddenly, still by the window. 'That must be him.'

A minute later someone was knocking on the door, although to the astonishment of everyone it was not the agent but Doña Soledad Ibañes herself and her nurse, whom she had brought along as a chaperone.

'D. Ramón,' she said politely, 'I apologize for the delay, but I have only just arrived from Madrid. I knew that you wished to give me the honour of authorising the document myself and did not wish to disappoint you on that.' And she went on haughtily, 'We can begin.'

D. Ramón flushed deeply. He felt furious but, at the same time, he saw that the vague hope he had always had – of seeing Doña Soledad again – was being realized. And, as is so often the case, he felt a sort of painful pleasure at his own humiliation.

The notary read out the clauses of the deed in the deliberate, incomprehensible and sombre voice that is so common to the representatives of his esteemed profession; this all done in the midst of the total lack of attention of those interested, which is also the custom.

D. Ramón was to give all his property to Doña Soledad, with the obligation on her part to recognize entire payment of all his debts to her.

Doña Soledad was the first to sign after which D. Ramón signed, summoning all his energy to write firmly.

'Madam,' D. Ramón said when the notary and witnesses had left, 'although you wanted the pleasure of coming personally to see the last representative of the Torrelavegas being thrown out of his home, I have to allow you one final satisfaction.' And, turning to Pedro, he told him, 'Go and call Carolina.'

Doña Soledad's eyes remained down, but D. Ramón looked directly at her.

'Carolina,' he said as the woman entered. 'Give the keys to this lady.'

'Carolina,' said Doña Soledad, raising her eyes, 'keep the keys.

41

Don't you want to remain as housekeeper in this house?'

'Madam,' Carolina declared, quietly dignified, 'my family has served the lords of Torrelavega for many hundreds of years. They came with them and they will leave with them.'

'Carolina,' Doña Soledad insisted, 'keep the keys. It isn't the Torrelavegas who are leaving – it's the Ibañes who are arriving.' And turning to everyone present she demanded, 'Leave me alone with D. Ramón.' When they had left she turned to him. 'D. Ramón, you discovered in a quarter of an hour that you were in love with me. As a woman I take things more slowly, but I am more constant in my feelings and reactions and have taken two months to be able to say the same regarding you. I love D. Ramón de Torrelavega, not the calculating D. Ramón who came searching me out but the poor and proud D. Ramón whom I have come here to find.'

A wave of happiness came over D. Ramón, a happiness that was poisoned by a persistent doubt. He was unable to dispel it and asked, tremulously,

'And what you told me about yourself?'

'Pure invention on my part.'

'How can I know that?'

'How can you know it? There's nothing more simple than a Castilian fidalgo! How can you know it?' She burst into delighted laughter. 'At the appropriate time, when you get full proof.'

'But that way,' D. Ramón objected with gentle irony, 'you're not keeping your promise to your father.'

'But I am,' she retorted, 'and with interest. I shan't have just D. Ramón's property, I'll have D. Ramón as well.'

Hardly had she said this than D. Ramón took her in his arms and kissed her on the lips as was, indubitably, the right thing to do.

§

D. Ramón de Torrelavega y Iglesias del Madrigal de las Torres Altas married Doña Soledad Ibañes, as you must have predicted. They married and were very happy. And so ends this true story, as so often happens in life, with a romantic ending which is nothing more than a sentimental cliché.

But is there any way of making everyone happy other than this?

The Hungarian Teacher

'I've always liked the idea of foreign languages,' the man said, 'particularly those that few or no people speak. I realize that it's a form of pride, but in a world where everyone has their vanities, many of which are humiliating or dangerous for others, it's perfectly inoffensive. So what do you think?'

Quite honestly, I didn't think anything, but since I felt I must sacrifice my indifference for the sake of courtesy, I feigned interest as I replied, 'I don't think that it's a matter of pride. It's primarily a desire to communicate in a certain way, a way to travel without the fatigue and expense of travel...'

I simply said this for the sake of something to say, just as I might have said any other thing, but he gladly latched onto my words.

'So right. So right!' he repeated. 'You have got to the root of the problem. You confirm what I've thought so often – it's only others who are able to work out the truth about what concerns us.'

There was no desire for flattery on his part, but I suddenly felt the need to curb his enthusiasm and so explained, 'When I say that it's inoffensive all I'm doing is pronouncing a very relative truth, because there are a few instances when speaking English well can be a matter of provocation. For example, I am always annoyed by people who speak foreign languages with perfect pronunciation because they always assume the air, even if they don't want to, of giving one a lesson or of criticizing one. Besides which – and here I fully support Eça de Queiroz when he states that one should have pride in speaking foreign languages

43

badly – to express oneself in such a way is a form of paying homage and a betrayal of our own language.'

The man listened to me attentively and agreed.

'Perhaps you're right. Yes, perhaps you're right. However, it's of no concern to me as you can't stick that one on me. I can speak a few foreign languages, but all badly, and I can even admit that there is one language no one has ever spoken worse than I.'

'Really?' I asked evasively.

He appeared to be paying no attention to my lack of concern and went on.

'It's a long story, but it's most illustrative. And perhaps it would interest you.'

'I'm sure it would.'

We were silent, and then he asked the absurd question, 'Do you speak Hungarian?'

'Hungarian?' I repeated. 'Hungarian? Why on earth would I speak Hungarian? Rather, what good would it do me?'

'A lot of good, or perhaps no good at all. It depends on the circumstances. That is, speaking it,' he went on pompously, 'is of no importance.'

'That's a stupid error,' I argued, determined to be difficult. 'A really stupid error, dangerously close to being ridiculed. There's nothing that is more important. But go on. Why did you have to speak Hungarian?'

He hesitated a moment and then replied so frankly that I was taken aback.

'I've already explained in part. And perhaps because of the idea I had – and it was a correct idea – that one day, for some reason, I should perhaps have to go to Hungary. And indeed I did go there. But that's not the reason for my story being so extraordinary.'

'So what was the reason?' I asked, now getting interested.

'It was the outcome of my learning.'

He had noted my interest and went on, obviously flattered, 'I'll tell you. One day I read an advertisement in a newspaper that said

Hungarian Teacher
Graduate of the University of Budapest
Will teach you to speak the most difficult language in the World

correctly and fluently in 50 lessons.
    10 sessions monthly: 1000$00. Group lessons 50% discount. X street, no. x, from 16h to 18h and 21h to midnight.

'I was amazed. A thousand escudos was far too much for me and I feared – though you will see later that I was wrong – that no one else in Portugal would want to learn Hungarian except for me. The following day after a sleepless, pensive night I decided to go looking for the teacher. I admit that I was nervous. The thought of meeting a Hungarian for the first time, though it might not seem so, needs a certain degree of courage. So I went up the five storeys of the old building that had no lift somewhat hesitantly.

'My first impression was, frankly, not pleasant. The house was sordid and the man no less so. I went into an enormous room with straw-bottomed chairs and a platform at the end that must once have been a dais for an old piano. This had without doubt been a dance club abandoned long ago.

' "Have you come to learn Hungarian?" the teacher asked abruptly.

'I timidly replied that that was the case.

' "You're the sixteenth person to come today. I never thought my wretched country would provoke such interest. *Atkozott akar.*"

' "What?" I asked. "I don't understand."

' "Of course you don't understand. It's Hungarian and it just means, *May they be cursed.*" Without pausing, he introduced himself somewhat pompously. "Count Igor Stienvensky, exile… and Hungarian teacher. And you are…?"

' "Isolino Pimenta, commercial salesman," I replied, embarrassed for some ridiculous reason.

' "Curious, very curious."

' "Why curious?"

' "Your surname. Portuguese surnames are very curious."

' "Why?" I asked.

' "Why? Because they come from every one of the nature's kingdoms. They're animals, or trees, or metals, or, as in your case, a spice. Today, for example, I had Sr. Iron, Sr. Lamb and Sr. Pear tree, etc., etc."

' "And what's wrong with that?" I asked, offended.

' "Nothing, nothing. It's just an observation."

'Once I had got over my shyness I looked at him directly. He was exceedingly tall, perhaps 1.90m, with straight, thin black hair and a drooping moustache. He was wearing an overall, or rather an old smock that was covered in stains and went down to his feet. One of his shoes had no lace and the other had a hole, displaying unquestionable poverty.

'The man guessed what I was thinking and explained quite naturally, "We noble Hungarians have spent our money to the last penny. It was only when we fell into total misery that we decided to work. That's what happened to me."

'He spoke Portuguese fluently, with a slight foreign accent that you could only notice when he pronounced his 'rr' and sometimes he got the gender of his nouns wrong.

'However, in spite of his poverty he had a certain dignity.

' "You speak Portuguese very well," I said, wanting to make amends for my rather rude curiosity.

' "You shouldn't be surprised, sir. I've been in Portugal since the first revolution, twelve years ago." And he went on rather proudly, "For a Hungarian you only need six months to learn a foreign language well. But foreigners can't manage to speak Hungarian in thirty years – rather, they never manage to learn it."

' "In that case," I remarked, "there's no point in giving lessons."

' "I'm talking about literary Hungarian, not everyday, essential Hungarian, which is what I teach. You can rest easy on that point. And if one day you should go to Hungary – which I would never wish on you – you will see how astonished they are at your Hungarian."

'It was only much later that I understood the subtle irony of this statement but in some way his words reassured me.

'He noticed this and asked, "When would you like to start your lessons?"

' "Tomorrow if possible."

' "Daytime or in the evening?"

' "In the evening. I work during the day."

'I was about to leave when he remarked, smiling, "There's just one small formality."

' "What's that?"

' "You must pay half a month's fees. It's customary."

' "Fine."

'I took out 250 escudos and gave it to him."

' "Group lessons, then?"

' "Yes, if there are others who want that."

'He smiled.

' "You may relax on that point. There are lots."

'And indeed there were.

'At the first lesson there were eleven of us, all looking at each other awkwardly, with that particular feeling you have when you're doing something out of the ordinary whose legitimacy – even though apparently innocent – might seem arguable to some people. Each of us secretly wanted to discover what had led the others to learn Hungarian. However, what was certain was that we had not yet built up a good enough relationship for this and each of us guarded his secret closely.

'We were all sitting on the straw-bottomed chairs in rows of five, and on all our faces there was a sort of fearful curiosity.

'From the platform, where there now stood a table and an arm-chair, the teacher shouted in a thunderous voice, "*Isten hozta nak a tietek haz*. Pupil number 1, repeat."

'Pupil number one repeated it, tongue-tied, mixing up his vowels and consonants.

'We all started to laugh.

' "Silence!" the teacher yelled. "Hungarian is a sacred language that doesn't allow for mockery. Now pupil 2."

'One by one we were all subjected to the same test. One of the bravest of us asked, "And what does it mean?"

' "You'll soon know. For the moment I'm doing a test, so that I can assess the ability of each of you. Now all together. Go on repeating it until I tell you to stop."

'The teacher stepped off the platform and walked up to us. Like a conductor of a choir who wants to find out who is singing out of tune he went up and down the rows listening carefully.

' "Horrible! Horrible! Pronunciation for which you should be shot." Then he continued in a conciliatory tone, "But as it's the first time, you're forgiven."

'Then he slowly went up to the blackboard and wrote the sentence in capital letters: *ISTEN HOZTA NAK A TIETEK HAZ*.

' "This is the easiest expression to pronounce in Hungarian. It's a commonly used salutation which is used every day and which simply means, "Welcome and please make yourself at home." Then without hesitation he added, "And now a warning. You are all forbidden for the moment to buy any dictionary. At this point it could only be a hindrance. And there is to be no thought of the Berlitz method. Never! I shall go on teaching you the vocabulary." In a ringing tone he went on, "*Honalpsig*, gentlemen." And he explained, "That means, "See you tomorrow""

'Utterly under his control, we all repeated together, "*Honalpsig*, Sir."

'It may seem odd to you,' Isolino Pimenta went on, 'that I am enjoying telling a story that is a little embarrassing for me, but the fact is that I like it.'

And so picking up the thread of his story he went on.

'The lessons carried on, with more and more people joining, and eventually there was a delightful element that was added to them – the presence of women. Some young girls had also decided to learn Hungarian. None of us knew why, nor perhaps did they. However, the fact is that they were more applied and even, as is usual, more diligent. I say this because, as you will see, this had a considerable effect, indeed a benefit, in my life, which perhaps goes to explain my later sense of goodwill. But to get to the matter. The eleven pupils we had originally been had become twenty-five and finally it was necessary to split us into two groups. Something had changed in the place and even in the teacher. The straw-bottomed chairs with holes were replaced by others that were more comfortable and the teacher's clothing had acquired a rather exotic elegance. He now appeared with velvet trousers and riding boots and a *rubask*, sometimes of blue silk, sometimes of red. His drooping moustache was glossy and he had a black lock of hair that was stuck to his forehead with the help of lacquer, all of which accentuated the Hungarian quality of his appearance. The teacher had won us over and quite naturally, without saying anything to each other (I believe that it was the girls who took the initiative on this, as they wanted to introduce a romantic element into the lessons) we began to address him as Count Igor, a homage he happily accepted as though it had always been his right. A gramophone, which played the Hungarian anthem on an old, scratched record, now marked the beginning and end of the lessons, and we listened to it standing respectfully – I was about to say we were moved by it – with the absurd but nonetheless real feeling of exiles from an unknown country. It was a "Longing for someone I have never seen..." of which the Poet spoke. The method he had adopted continued to be that of the first lesson. We would speak the words or sentences individually and then repeat them in chorus. In some way the course was like ones held in Arab schools, when they chant the verses of the Koran together. All that we lacked was being seated on mats with our legs crossed. What was certain, though, was that the system had its results. Although there were difficulties in pronunciation, at which our teacher was most demanding (he would make us repeat a word dozens of times), we could understand each other perfectly and when we met in the street we would greet each other in the Hungarian our teacher had taught us. Unconsciously a brotherhood had been created among us which, because of its air of mystery, gave us standing and importance. For us it was exciting when we met in a café to speak in this exotic language, much to the surprise – and admiration – of the other customers.

'"I am teaching you," insisted the teacher, "Hungarian for human interaction, what the ordinary people speak. I want you to know how to say everything necessary for essential communication."

'And the fact is that he fully achieved this. So much so that one of our joys was to murmur sweet words to our female colleagues, words which seemed to abound in the Hungarian language. For my part, I confess that this was how I said to my wife – at the time my classmate – for the first time, that I loved her: '*Szerelem* (my love), I whispered, to which she replied lovingly, "*Szerelem*".

'I apologize for telling you all this, as it's a little shocking, but the fact is that it is necessary for a complete understanding of my tale. And I also have to confess, although it's hard to admit it, that in spite of what happened later, we still sometimes use those endearments when we are alone. When the course was coming to an end (there were more and more people turning up and the teacher had too much on his hands), the unexpected chance arrived that would justify *a posteriori* my desire to learn Hungarian.

'The director of the firm where I worked, and of which I am now a partner, called me to his office one morning and in a rather solemn voice, in which there was clearly some concern, he said, "Listen, Pimenta, I'm going to make a proposition to you which you may or may not accept. If you don't, I shan't be angry and it won't prejudice your career. However, if you accept it would be wonderful for the firm and for you, particularly since, as you are the longest standing employee here and the most well-informed, I could only ask you to carry out the task."

'He was quiet for a moment and then went on, "As you know, although Portugal has no diplomatic relations with Iron Curtain countries, we have commercial agreements with Czechoslovakia and Hungary which are guaranteed by a clearing. Now I know that, particularly in Hungary following the last revolution, there is a great need for plastics. So there is a fantastic opportunity for us to place our products there. Would you like to go to Hungary as our representative?"

'My heart skipped a beat and I turned pale. Did the directors of the firm know that I had been learning Hungarian and was this simply putting me to the test, as they say?

'But this thought was soon dispelled, firstly because he wasn't that kind of man and secondly because of his reaction when he saw how surprised I was.

' "Look, man, if you have any qualms, don't think about it any more. I'll go…"

' "I've no qualms at all," I said decisively.

' "Well, are you worried about the language? If you are, you shouldn't be concerned. Almost everyone speaks French and English in Hungary, and you speak both well."

' "It's nothing to do with the language." And with a degree of pride I went on, "As well as speaking French and English I also know a little Hungarian."

' "Hungarian?" Now it was the director's turn to be surprised and with a slightly distrustful tone, as though wanting to discover the reason for such an absurd thing, he repeated, "Hungarian? Why on earth did you learn Hungarian?"

' "Just by chance," I replied. "I read an advertisement placed by a Hungarian teacher and decided to learn without any thought except to learn it. And now it looks as though I did the right thing."

'The director's face brightened.

' "Perfect. Excellent. So much the better. So you accept?"

' "I do. But I think I need a special permit!"

' "Yes, you do, but I'll deal with that, so don't worry. When do you think you can leave?"

' "Whenever you want."

'The director was most happy, shook my hand and we parted. I was over the moon. My decision had, after all, been justified. And I couldn't even feel concern at having spent my money to no purpose, as I was going to recuperate it. My first task that afternoon was to go and buy a dictionary. It was the final month of the lessons and, contrary to what the teacher thought, this could do me no harm at this point. I went to all the bookshops to no avail, without finding what I wanted. It was only at the last one that they told me they had had a copy some time earlier.

' "We sold it about six months ago," the assistant said, "and I think it was to a Hungarian. It was the only copy."

'I was annoyed, although it wasn't really important. I already knew enough Hungarian to get by. I knew, or thought I knew, which comes to the same thing.

'That night – when we were having our penultimate lesson – I told my colleagues and the teacher what had happened. They all congratulated me loudly - all except, that is, the teacher, who shook his head with a sad air and said, "Come and see me at the end of the lesson."

'I thought that he wanted to give me some advice, and after my colleagues left I went to see him. The teacher looked at me like someone staring at a man condemned to a life sentence and asked in a gloomy voice, "Tell me the truth. Are you really going to Hungary or are you teasing me?"

' "Absolutely!" I said, and told him what had happened.

' "If I were you I shouldn't go," he said firmly. "And although it hurts me to say it about my country, I must warn you that nowadays, in the state it's in, it's not the place for civilized people."

' "I promised that I would go, and I'm going," I said firmly. "Not everyone can be hurt by them, and they're not going to eat me."

' "That's what you think. But as you've promised, go. But just do me one favour."

' "Tell me. Whatever you want," I replied, thinking that he was going to ask me to bring back some souvenir and contact someone.

' "At least… at least don't speak Hungarian, and even pretend that you have no idea how to speak it."

' "Why?" I asked, surprised.

' "Because since Hungarian is a language hardly anyone speaks they will think that you are a spy. And the best that could happen to you is you would be imprisoned or… or…" and he went on sinisterly, "summarily shot. Promise you won't?"

'In order to reassure him, and touched by his enormous interest in my personal safety and physical wellbeing, I solemnly promised, "Don't worry; I shan't speak Hungarian."

'But I was determined not to keep my promise…'

§

'I crossed the Austro-Hungarian border with no problem,' Isolino Pimenta went on, 'My papers were in order and the management of the company had dealt with everything correctly. Both the police and the customs officials spoke to us in French and English, which was probably understandable since there wasn't a single Hungarian in the carriage in which I had been travelling. They were all foreigners, tourists or businessmen like me. None of them spoke Hungarian.

'"It's an impossible language!" a French travelling salesman told me. "Even they say that Hungarian can't be learned after the age of three. And as far as I'm concerned, that's true. I've already been here three or four times and I can't understand a word."

' "Well I can say a bit," I ventured timidly. "Well, let's say I know a little."'

'The Frenchman looked me up and down and replied, smiling, "*Excusez-moi, monsieur… Mais je m'en doute.*"

'I didn't press the point.

'It was only when I reached the hotel that I decided to demonstrate my Hungarian.

' "*Kivan egy zzoba* (I'd like a room)," ' I said, clearly pronouncing the words.

'The porter looked at me surprised.

' "*Kivan egy zzoba*," ' I repeated.

' "*Comprend pas*. I don't understand…"

'At that point the thought of the teacher's warning came to my mind. "Oh hell," I thought, "I've been stupid." From my accent he had realized that I was foreign and didn't want to give himself away. Hotel porters are often from the police and no one knows the instructions they've been given.

' *"Je voulais une chambre."*
' *"Très bien. Pour combien de jours?"*
' *"Cinq ou six."*
'The conversation continued in French.

'The porter asked me for my documents, examined them meticulously and made me sign the hotel register.

'Finally he asked me what time I wanted to get up.

' "At seven," I replied.

'I like to get up early and walk round the cities which are new to me so that I can learn more about them. Besides which, I would have the chance to come into contact with the people, those who don't speak any other language, so that I could try out my Hungarian without any fear or police restrictions.

'I spent the whole morning walking round the magnificent city where, by now, there were hardly any of the signs of the terrible revolution that had made it a blood bath. It was a wonderful morning, but it was also disappointing.

'On the pretext of asking where this or that place was I approached some people in the street in Hungarian. They stopped attentively, listened to me with a certain air of surprise and said something which I didn't understand.

' "Well now," I thought, "either they don't understand my Hungarian or I'm the one who doesn't understand theirs." I determined upon the second of these hypotheses. "Right, I must be the one whose ear isn't attuned." But I began to feel a lack of confidence, although this wasn't fixed but was, nevertheless, insistent. "I've got to sort this out, whatever the outcome."

'That afternoon I had a meeting set up with the head of the branch that was interested in buying my products, and I determined to do an experiment. Notwithstanding the risk I ran (and by now I was beginning to believe that I did run a risk, the more so since this was at a government office), I made the decision to talk to him in Hungarian and only Hungarian.

'And so once I had made the decision, I was determined on it.

'For five minutes, to the evident astonishment and open mouths of those present (the head of the department was accompanied by two technical advisers) I spoke Hungarian, only Hungarian, my Hungarian, acquired by the sweat of my brow, that I had so wanted to learn and

53

that had cost me so much in time and money.

'I have a suspicion that if the man hadn't interrupted me rather rudely, I would still be speaking Hungarian.

' "Do you not speak another language?" he asked in perfect French. And he went on, "I don't understand the language you're using."

' "I do speak French, but tell me something. Aren't you Hungarian?" I asked, clinging to my last hope.

' "Of course I am. Why?"

' "It's just that..." I said, hesitating a little. "It's just that I was speaking in Hungarian, or rather *I thought I was speaking in Hungarian.*"

' "Your thinking is wrong. It could perhaps be Kurdish, Swedish or Basque, whatever you choose. What it isn't is Hungarian."

' "Are you sure?"

' "Absolutely. Who told you it was?"

'Although I was embarrassed, I told them the tale of my lessons in order to explain my behaviour. The man laughed uproariously. From time to time he would speak in a language I didn't recognize to his companions, who didn't speak French, and they joined in the laughter.

'Suddenly they fell silent.

' "Wait there," the head of the department said as though having an idea. "Write something down *in your Hungarian.*"

'I didn't hesitate and wrote a long sentence.

'The man looked and looked again, then smiled.

' "Now tell me what it means."

'I immediately obeyed.

' "That's what I thought," he went on. "The words are Hungarian and the spelling is right. It's simply that the man who taught you didn't know the tenses of the verbs or the syntax or, most of all, it would seem, the pronunciation. You and your companions have been the victims of a trick."

'And not wanting to waste this opportunity for propaganda, he went on pompously, "That's something that could only happen in a capitalist country."

' "What a scoundrel," I shouted, furious.

' "Is that Hungarian too?" he asked ironically.

' "No, it's Portuguese, and it means *Quel salaud*"

'I was so angry that I don't know how I managed to carry on with the business in hand. However, I did, and it all went well. But the fact that I did, I'm sure now, is because they were interested in pursuing it.

'The knowledge that I had been tricked remained with me. "The trickster!" I thought. "As well as taking my money he was making fun of me." And the thought that other people had fallen for the same hoax was no consolation. On the contrary – it made me still more angry. I thought of us talking to each other in idiotic words, thoroughly convinced, while he was laughing at the group of idiots that we were. I'm very sensitive to ridicule and this filled me with fury. Now everything was becoming clear and I understood why he had forbidden us from buying dictionaries – he, who had bought the only Hungarian dictionary to be found in the Lisbon bookshops. And that was the dictionary for sure – the source of his slight knowledge – that had suggested to him the idea of his fraudulent behaviour.

"The bastard!" I murmured to comfort myself, although I had come to a firm decision. "You wait until I get to Lisbon and then you'll pay, as sure as my name is Isolino Pimenta,"

Furious, and robbed of all the delight at my commercial success, as a source of consolation I decided to spend the evening at one of those rare cabarets that could still be found on the banks of the Danube. There, to the sound of Monti's Czardas played by an orchestra comprising fake *tziganos*, I could really become intoxicated with Hungary.

§

'When I got back to Lisbon,' Isolina Pimenta went on, 'my work didn't allow for me to go looking for the teacher immediately. My trip to Hungary and its commercial success meant that I had realized one of my old ambitions – to be made a partner, although with a small shareholding. My capability regarding international commerce was now indisputable and although I didn't confess to it (something I would never do), my partners would not have believed how useless and pointless my being involved had been. Indeed Senhor Carvalho, the head of the firm, even in my presence would say to anyone who wanted to hear it, "Our Pimenta here is brilliant when it comes to matters of export," leaving me somewhat embarrassed.

'However none of this diminished my anger at the teacher or lessened my desire for justified revenge. "If I manage to get him he'll soon see..."

'During the return journey I had thought deeply about the problem and resolved to abandon my original idea of going to the police. However, the fact that I had abandoned it wasn't out of kindness or generosity but simply in order for me to avoid a humiliating situation. I could already see the "officers", with that look that belongs so entirely to them, staring at me with that superior disdain they use when looking at idiots who believe in the philosopher's stone.

' "No," I thought, "it's something that must be resolved directly with a couple of punches. As for the money, I don't give a damn. I'll behave as though I had gambled it away."

'I had also hesitated about telling my classmates what had happened, as I wanted to catch the teacher unawares. If I had met them I don't know whether I would have had the courage, and it's a fact that two months after returning from Hungary I hadn't seen any of them. It was as though they had vanished!

'Anyway, my trip had improved my situation, leading to my being able to realize one of my greatest desires – to marry. However, I did decide to tell my future wife what had happened.

'She listened to me in thoughtful silence and as I waited for an indignant outburst, instead she broke into a loud laugh. "What a wonderful trick! What a joke," she said, in fits of laughter.

'Women don't usually forgive anyone who uses them and they also don't usually have a very sharp sense of humour. So her attitude made me even more furious.

' "You think so? You think so? Well, I'll tell you this. When I find him I'll tear him to pieces. Be sure of it, I'll kill him."

' "You're wrong," she said, becoming serious again. "You're completely wrong, because although he did you an injury, you owe him – modesty apart – enormous gratitude."

' "What's that? Would you kindly tell me?"

' "Getting to know me," she said, "as if it weren't for him we would never have met. So as far as I'm concerned, I'm very grateful to him."

' "Very true, but all the same it doesn't excuse his behaviour. You can think what you want, but I'll never forgive him for having robbed me and, worst of all, for having ridiculed me and, admit it, ridiculed you too."

' "Well, I forgive him."

'Her argument was certainly logical, and so I came to a decision, although I didn't tell her – I wouldn't assault him, but I would denounce him.

'And when I make a decision I stick to it.

'One night I would go to one of his lessons and during that puppet show I would denounce him. I felt that this was a moral duty on my part, an obligation towards the others which I couldn't avoid.

'In spite of this, I hesitated for a few days, but one evening after thinking hard as to what I was going to say, at the exact time of the lessons I went up the five flights of stairs in the old building with a determined step.

'However, fate would have it that that was not to be the night when I would get my revenge.

'For more than a quarter of an hour I beat pointlessly and furiously on the door. I beat it so loudly and made such a noise that the neighbour who lived to the left came out, startled, to ask what was going on.

' "What do you want? Who are you looking for?"

' "A great liar who lives here," I replied angrily. "A guy who calls himself Count Igor Stievensky."

' "Lives here! No – he did live here," the ugly-looking neighbour said. "He disappeared one fine day without paying his rent. And now, let me sleep, please. I work and have to get up early. Good night!"

'Without further ceremony he shut the door in my face.

'I went down the stairs slowly and as I did a great calm took over me and I thought, "Well, someone obviously found the cheat out and decided to send him on his way. Right, that's the end of it."

'A long time went by, maybe a year or more, from the time I was talking about. Meanwhile my economic situation was improving all the time and I had married. I was happy and happiness leads to benevolence. I could even speak about the teacher with my wife without getting angry. No one had seen him since – not me or my old classmates, whom I put straight on the matter as and when I met them. However, the majority didn't believe what I told them, though this didn't concern or offend me.

'I believed the matter closed and indeed wasn't thinking any more about it. But man proposes and God disposes. One night, during one of my trips to those old corners of Lisbon which I so enjoy visiting, Fate came once again to prove to me that it is stronger than man.

'I was looking, entranced, at one of the old mouldings with a coat of arms above it that give a certain medieval cachet to our beautiful city when, as I lowered my eyes, I saw in the dubious, smoky light of a bar, a shape with its back to me, a shape that wasn't entirely unknown to me.

'I looked more carefully and my heart skipped a beat. My God, who was it? No more nor less than the teacher, with his tall bent body, the teacher once more restored to his original, proper misery and his old stained overall.

'I confess that I felt no anger, but rather – strange though it may seem – a sort of tenderness. After hesitating for a moment, when I went into the bar I did so not to denounce him but as someone wanting to revive an old relationship with a long-lost friend.

'"Hello there!" I said, slapping him on the back.

'The teacher turned round, surprised. When he recognized me, his face lit up.

'"Hello, hello my dear friend!" And there was a simple, sincere delight in his eyes. "Well, look who it is!"

'And everything would have carried on like that with a hug and possibly a couple of 'stiff ones' together if he hadn't had the foolish idea of recalling that he was a count and a Hungarian teacher.

'"Oh my dear friend! *Hanem micsoda nagi öröm! Micsoda nagi öröm, szretett barati!*"

'"Oh no, count! Oh no! For God's sake, stop that babble."

'But he was letting loose, pronouncing muddled sentences in that unintelligible language.

'As he was talking, so my old, long-gone anger was welling up in me, becoming more vehement and violent. "Oh you bastard!" I thought, "you still want to trick me. You'll see!"

'I grabbed him by both arms and, with my face almost touching his, yelled at him,

'"Shut up, you fool. Shut up, otherwise I'll smash your face in."

'And to the astonishment of those around us I told him what had happened, saying everything that came to mind.

'The man remained upright and unmoved and his face took on an expression of righteous disappointment.

'"It seems to me impossible that you should say such things to me. To me, your friend and teacher. To me, who taught you classical Hungarian, the noble, true Hungarian! I find it impossible that you didn't understand me!"

'Astonished, I let go of him.

' "So what didn't I understand, Sir?"

' "What? What? *Atkozotts*! *Atkozotts*. You didn't understand that it was entirely their fault. They are the ones who tricked you, not me! Bastards! What they've done to my wretched country! Bastards! They've changed everything. Everything, even the language and the pronunciation! *Isten vele*! Goodbye!"

'And with his arms raised, muttering incomprehensible words, he disappeared into the night darkness.'

Sleep

'What's just happened to you is the best thing that can happen to a man after a few years of living with one woman. Are you telling me she's left you? Perfect.'

Pedro started in disgust and indignation.

'You're forgetting that I loved her and that I still love her.'

'No, I'm not forgetting, just as I'm not forgetting the slightly wounded pride that such a thing causes even to those as used to it as I am.'

'As you?' Pedro asked in astonishment. 'I always imagined that you were happy when it comes to women. At least that's what people say.'

'And it's absolutely true. I'm extremely happy when it comes to women. And the reason is, simply and precisely, not because I'm an irresistible ladies' man but because they were always the ones who took the initiative and left me.'

'I don't understand.'

The two fell silent. From the veranda of the house, which was covered in white wisteria, one could see the Tagus and Mouchão da Póvoa. Some boats were heading for the banks, their sails down. The wind had suddenly dropped and they were looking for protection against the current. The sun was going down and tinged the distant Palmela hill a pale red.

'See?' Luís said to his friend, without replying directly to his remark. 'There's always a moment when the wind drops and when, every day, the sun sinks relentlessly below the horizon. Those sails that were billowing and proud just a while ago are empty now, while the men find themselves forced to row their boats to the banks. But tomorrow the sun will rise again and there will be wind once more. They know that, and so they don't complain. That's how life is. That's how love is. It's just that you didn't know and, instead of preparing for your destiny, you were surprised by it.'

'I've already told you that I love her.'

'I do see, and I understand better than anyone your raw bitterness. But I also know that, in spite of that, you are paying a small price for the great good fortune that's smiled upon you.'

His friend signalled his disagreement and was about to reply when Luís went on.

'Listen, Pedro. I know you as well as I know myself, indeed I know a large number of men. There would have come a time when it would have been you who stopped loving her, which would be far worse than what's happened now. You know, in love – and it's repeated over and over again like every truth that is easily proved – what's important is loving, not being loved. That's because only the one who loves can feel the deep, almost divine happiness caused by love. And then – what would you do?'

'Then the matter would be easy to resolve.'

'Oh no it wouldn't. The result would be just the same – either you would enter into a life of tolerance and compromise – which is what the majority of men do – but which permanently excludes love, which isn't in your nature, or you would have to desert her with all the consequences of such behaviour. For a man who has self-respect – listen to me – a man who has self-respect never leaves a woman who loves him.'

'Have you never left a woman?'

'No, I've never left a woman who loved me. That's how I've managed to keep not just a clear conscience but also the esteem of almost all of them, which is a precious gift. There was one time though, when I was tempted to do it – a terrible time for me, when I'd run out of all avenues and found myself almost forced to behave in a way which I deeply condemn and for which I would never have forgiven myself. What saved me at the last minute was my deep knowledge of the psychology and, in particular, of the nature of women. You must know that it's always much easier to conquer a woman than to make a woman who loves us turn against us and decide to leave us. But, as I said, there was a moment in my life when I was at risk of getting it wrong. That was when...'

'That was when?...' Pedro repeated, forgetting his emotional problem and suddenly interested.

'About six years ago, when faced with the unshakeable love women have when they draw new forms of endurance from all the misfortune and unhappiness men cause them...'

'But that's the ideal for any man,' Pedro said. 'That would have been my ideal.'

'No, Pedro, in the majority of cases – except when you find *the* woman (and I've never found her!) – it's simply horrible. When a man can't respond to that kind of love it's as though you've set up a current account and the overdraft is always getting bigger. There's a problem there, a permanent disloyalty that's bound up in every action, which not even the apparent love they're faking can justify. And that was precisely what happened to me. Do you remember Antonieta?'

'A brunette with green eyes you went out with for a while? I think that you introduced her to me. But I can only vaguely remember her.'

'That's the one. Well, although she was what you'd call an easy conquest, she was the most difficult woman in my life. It all began like those things always begin, driven on by man's desire and that vague sentiment women call affection. I'm not saying that there wasn't tenderness on my part, tenderness, that tenderness that I'm always happy to give every woman who, as a woman, is worthy of it. Put simply, neither my past nor, particularly, hers, allowed for such a sentiment. Antonieta was what you'd call shallow, even frivolous – and deservedly so – which I didn't notice, as a woman's past was out of bounds and sacred as far as I was concerned. So, as I believed what she said and as the past is somehow a guarantee of the future, when I began things with her I was prepared (and deep down – why not admit it? – I was even hoping) to take all the consequences. All the consequences, that is, all those that I could logically expect given my initial impression. Put simply, the only thing I couldn't have counted on happened – that of my being for her the one and only man. Gradually I began to realise this and I admit that at the beginning, being vain, I was flattered, although the agreeable awareness of this phenomenon was very soon shaken by a slight sense of danger which always takes hold of me when I'm confronted by cosmic forces of nature. Because when love takes on that aspect and assumes that intensity it becomes an almost invincible cosmic force. Without my really realizing it, that woman was taking up all my time, indeed my life, and doing it in a shrewd, subtle way by constantly conforming to my likes, habits and whims. Even when it came to my work, which she didn't comprehend as she was incapable of any artistic understanding, she would lean over me with interested, tender solicitude. For a lot of people this wouldn't appear more than a conversion to a new idea of life, but I knew that wasn't the case! I knew that it was merely love, extreme love, that love that is capable of every form of understanding. However, it wasn't then that I began to be worried and in fact I started to accept her dedication as some kind of homage, at times a nuisance but always delightful. I only became consciously frightened by it when I realized that Antonieta's affection for me had acquired the most terrible and inescapable form that feminine love can assume – contemplative love. A woman's love is always more direct than that of men, more sensitive to situations and occurrences and therefore more vulnerable. However when, through a sort of sublimation, it reaches those heights when human behaviour has no repercussions, then it becomes invulnerable and intangible. And that's what terrified me.

'One night I woke suddenly and saw her green eyes wide open, staring lovingly at me. "What's up?" I asked sleepily. "Nothing; I just like looking at you when you're asleep. You look like a little boy. I spend ages doing that."

'That was when I became aware of the danger threatening me and it was also then that I subconsciously made the decision to get her out of my life. It's true that at the time my desire for her had faded, had slipped into the ways of married life, and I had already expressed to her (I was the one, not she, who always came up with new ideas and new expressions) every loving word, always the same (amorous vocabulary is the smallest of all), it is only later that they become a matter of meaningless repetition when spoken with no feeling. So I started confidently to establish a plan, although I knew from much experience that the task was not going to be easy. On the other hand I confess that I didn't think it would be quite so difficult.'

'But wouldn't it have been easier, more dignified, to tell her of your lack of interest, which after all wasn't your fault?' Pedro interrupted, slightly irritated. 'More loyal and even more honest?'

'Don't be so childish, Pedro, and just think of your own situation.

As you've already told me, Berra was loyal to you, but that loyalty necessarily presupposes a lack of love and interest, which you find hard to forgive. And after all you're a man, no more intelligent and no stronger than a woman, but more logical and rational. The only loyalty due to a woman is not to disappoint her in what, to her, is fundamental – our love. When a woman falls in love with a man – when she really is in love with him, of course – she's prepared for anything: the sacrifices, the betrayals and even being treated badly. She may even accept a separation at some point even though this might be against her wishes. The only thing that she can't accept, which deep down in her conscience she tirelessly rejects, is that someone would leave her because he wasn't interested in her any more, because he doesn't love her. That's the only thing that truly hurts and humiliates her. So this is something a man mustn't do and something I shall never do. Man's duty is quite the opposite: to suggest an everlasting love – to suggest, take note, but not to promise, because promises to women, just like promises to children, must be faithfully adhered to, even though one might not be prepared to accept the resulting obligations. But let's get to the point. Once I'd made up my mind in the face of a love that by its persistence was becoming more and more disturbing, I decided to attempt what, to me, seemed the most practical solution which, in the case of a certain number of women, is the easiest: jealousy and brutality. I waited for an opportunity and this came up thanks to one of those sentimental romantic American films full of tacky images that cannot fail to impress a passionate, sensitive woman. During one of the most meaningful scenes when the hero took the woman in his arms and then threw himself *delicately* on a bale of straw with her, I began to sense Antonieta's breast rising and falling and her hand grabbed my wrist in an unconscious suggestion that she'd like to repeat with me what was going on on the screen. I roughly took away my arm and when it was time for the interval, unlike what I usually do, which is to go out with her to have a bit of a walk and see the clothes in the foyer windows, I got up quickly and with an "I'm going to have a cigarette," murmured between my teeth I left the cinema without giving her time to follow. Several times up to the end of the film she tried to get close to me, either putting her arm on mine or with her loving fingers gently squeezing my hand that was tightly clenching the edge of the seat. But each time I pushed her away as though I had been the victim of some terrible offence. After the film, in the car, faced with

64

my obstinate silence which I continued, and my furrowed brow, she couldn't stop herself asking, "What's wrong with you, Luís?" "What's wrong with me? You're asking me that? What a cheek..."

'I put my foot down on the pedal, accelerated rapidly and drove to Monsanto at a ridiculous speed. I suddenly stopped there, where we were surrounded by brambles and shrubs and looked at her with a look filled with mysterious and terrible accusations. "What's wrong with you, Luís. What have I done?" she asked with that delightful feminine discomfort when they are confronted with the harsh, mysterious anger of the male. "Nothing, absolutely nothing." And I grasped her wrists, tightening my grip on them as though a wave of fury had taken hold of my senses and my muscles. "Nothing. You liked the film, didn't you? You really enjoyed it? You'd have liked to be," and at this point I spelled out the words with such anger that my voice was rising and becoming more and more real, "you'd really have liked to be the heroine, wouldn't you?" "What heroine?" Antonieta whispered. "What heroine?" "You're pretending not to know...The one Gregory Peck threw onto the bale of straw... Wouldn't you?" "You're out of your mind!" she replied in surprise. "Oh, really? Well I'll tell you this: lying down with some other man or lying down with Gregory Peck in your thoughts is the same thing..." "You're mad!" "Shut up," I went on. "Love is like God, when we sin against Him in thought, word and deed... And for me an actual betrayal is just the same as your betrayal... Do you know what you are?" "What am I?" she asked, raising her voice. And she repeatedly angrily, "Go on, tell me, what do you think I am?" "A sinner, a real sinner." "What you want," she said furiously "is for me to say you're right. But don't sit around waiting..." I grasped her wrists roughly and then, as though I had reached the peak of my fury, I hit her. "Bastard!" she hissed, her voice ringing out like an anomaly in the scented silence of the evening, and then she went on, "Take me home!" Without another word I obeyed and slowly drove down the hill. I confess that I wasn't pleased with myself: hitting a woman is something I abhor. I had only done it because I remembered what she had said about a friend of hers, "I don't know how Elisa puts up with that man... If a man ever laid his hands on me, however much I liked him, I'd never speak to him again." At the door of her house she didn't hold out her hand, but said coldly, "Don't call me again, Luís. It's over between us." "Whatever you want!" I replied in the same tone. And I went down the road, not with a clear conscience but with that agreeable though disturbed state of mind of someone who has closed a book of which the best passages will be remembered some day but which has already revealed its secret in its entirety...

'The trouble was that contrary to what I was assuming, the final chapter hadn't yet been read, and two days later I received a letter from her, which I opened in the hope that it would contain written confirmation of her verbal decision. But no. The letter read:

> *Darling*
> *I have just kissed the marks you made on my wrists. Now, yes. Now I'm certain, because of your jealousy, although it was unjustified, that you really love me. Come to me darling! Come, before I die of longing...*

'I screwed up the letter and threw it on the floor. However, faithful to my principle of never disappointing a woman in what is, for them, fundamental – the certainty of our love – I obeyed. With my attempts frustrated, the only thing I had managed to do was raise the temperature of her feelings and make her love more insistent and more of a nuisance. All the same, I had made up my mind. So my jealousy hadn't worked? I'd work on hers, then. Some time after our reconciliation I called on Ruth, a girlfriend I'd had when I was young, one of those women you can trust implicitly in spite of her adventurous lifestyle, and I told her at once, "Ruth, you're going to do me a favour. Call this blasted woman and tell her that, being the louse that I am, I'm having lunch tomorrow in Montes Claros between one and two with a woman I'm in love with. And tell her that you feel sorry for her and you know what she feels about me but you've decided you must tell her, etc...etc... You know what to say, don't you?" "Fine, and then?" "Then tomorrow you're going to have lunch with me between one and two at Montes Claros." "You're shameless! Absolutely shameless! I shouldn't do it for you, because it's a betrayal of my sex, but as I know that you're really quite nice and because of certain things in the past" – and here she looked at me meaningfully –"I'll happily do it. But if you get me involved in a scene..." "Don't worry, there'll be no scene. She's not that type of woman." "I know, you want to upset her." "Yes, kind of."

'The next day everything went according to plan. At about one forty-five Antonieta appeared. She looked round the room and as soon as I saw her coming in I pretended to be embarrassed and hid my face behind a newspaper. She stopped beside our table and totally ignoring the woman who was with me simply said, "Good afternoon, Luís. Would you please come with me?" I stood up pretending to be uncomfortable, which I was in fact feeling, as even though the situation had been planned it was still embarrassing, and muttered, "Well you can see... Now... it's not possible. You..." And I gestured as though about to introduce the woman who was with me. "Yes, I can see, I can see perfectly well. I'm not blind." And without looking back she walked across the dining room and got in the taxi that was waiting for her at the door.

'I have to admit that this expedient left a nasty taste in my mouth and I had only decided to turn to it as a last resort. I'm a one-woman man and I don't like people to think otherwise. I might have different women in succession, but I'm never unfaithful to them. However, this was necessary, and when something is necessary I don't hesitate.

'The next day, counting on the success of the plan, I wrote her a letter giving her an explanation – an untruthful explanation which by its nature not even a child would have accepted, but being careful to emphasize my deep, unshakeable love for her – in spite of my supposed dalliance. This to me is a sure way not simply to preserve a woman's pride but also to gain her complete pardon at a later date.

'For a fortnight I had no news of her and assumed that I was free, and started making plans for a trip abroad, when I received a reply; and what an impassioned reply! In it she not only forgave my actions and the fact that I was capable of behaving like that, but she begged me to return to her, threatening to kill herself otherwise. And the letter ended – to think how women have been educated and brought up! – with a sentence from *The Memoirs of the Marquis of Bradomin,* of Valle-Inclán: Now my darling I feel it to be true "that the person who has never known the divine pleasure of timorous reconciliation has never known true love..."

'I was appalled, but true to my principles and the logic of my conviction I went back to her.

'For a few days which anyone else might have considered a delightful reconciliation but which for me was a complete nightmare, I meditated long and hard on the problem. Antonieta's affection had intensified and there was now a new driving force – the thought of competition increased her solicitude and sharpened her amorous imagination. We lived separately, but with her constant telephone calls, her surprise visits, her uncalled-for enthusiasm that was manifest in every possible way, I felt my privacy being invaded and my need for solitude greatly disturbed, since if I don't have my space I become one man too many among other men.

'Things couldn't carry on this way and it was precisely at that moment that I was almost prepared to write her a letter telling her callously that I wasn't interested in her. One scruple stopped me though – a scruple that arose from the combination of ideas and sentiments that had always led me to act differently and that I found difficult to overcome. It was then that the idea came to my head to put to use the plans for my trip abroad, which would make me more comfortable in myself. Simple ideas, which are those that usually have the best results, are also those that are more difficult to come across. Up until then I had hoped to get to her through her feelings, her psychological make-up. Why not try to attack her womanly qualities instead, as we all know that women, with their habits and needs, are far more protective of their prerogatives and rights?

'The idea was simply to disturb her habits, those that, whether justified or not, she declared were necessary for the preservation of her health and youth. From that moment I decided to put the idea into practice, cloaking my duplicitous intentions in the most attractive of pretexts. "Antonieta," I said to her that afternoon, "I need to go to Spain and France to do some research on the baroque influence on western architecture. Would you like to come with me? I do have to warn you that it's going to be a tiring trip. We'll have to travel a lot and you wouldn't be able to sleep as much as you do in Portugal."

'Antonieta grabbed at the idea with both hands. "Oh, darling, that doesn't matter at all. When I'm with you nothing tires me." A wave of happiness coloured her cheeks and I, knowing what I was preparing, felt (as I still do) a slight sense of remorse when faced with such effusive and sincere delight. "Darling, it's going to be wonderful!"

'The trip would fulfil one of my dearest, deepest desires. Antonieta was a free woman, but she liked to retain her composure and keep up appearances. So our life together was limited and surrounded by a thousand and one factors. On a trip – and this is what particularly interested her – our intimacy could be complete and she could take total control of me, suck the life from me down to the marrow.

'Three days later we left and, for two weeks, under the scorching August sun we crossed Spain from north to south and east to west, without sparing her a museum, a beautiful view, a cathedral and even sometimes a simple altar piece in a mountain hermitage. From the Giralda tower in Seville, which I made her climb five times in two days under a variety of pretexts, to the mosque in Cordoba, where we spent hours in 40-degree heat, I remorselessly forced her to see everything, so that we admired Our Lady of the Pillar in Saragossa, the Municipal Chambers in Astorga, while in Valladolid it was St Paul's gate and in León the palace of D. Juan Quiñones y Gusmán. During that fortnight we travelled six thousand kilometres, visited thirty-four cathedrals, went to twenty-one museums and climbed eighteen hills, at times on foot up steep routes, in order to enjoy eighteen magnificent viewpoints. Meanwhile I made sure that I didn't allow her to sleep more than three hours a night. We would go to bed late, because I frequently had the urge to go either to a theatre to see a zarzuela or to a ballet, and I would then roughly wake her at five in the morning (in Lisbon she would never get up before midday) in order to leave on another journey of hundreds of kilometres, which I told her was necessary for my research. Antonieta could stand it no longer and I could see that her exhaustion was slowly turning to silent irritation and occasionally I glimpsed fleeting but evident flashes of hatred. At night, when she went to bed, she'd forget to give me a simple kiss and when I woke her in the morning she would mutter words which were incomprehensible but which must have been expressing her absolute fury. Her defiance occurred, explosively, when we were in Madrid, the day before we were due to leave for France, when I suggested we should go to Trujillo. "And how many kilometres is that from here?" "It's close. About five hundred kilometres there and back." "Very close," she said sarcastically. "And here you are, the day before we go to France, wanting us to take some boring trip like that?" "Trujillo, Antonieta, is the birthplace of Pizarro," I told her solemnly. "You know who Pizarro is?" "No, I don't know and I don't want to know. I've lived thirty-two years in ignorance and I hope to remain that way." "Pizarro," I told her severely, "was one of the greatest Spanish conquistadores. His influence on Latin-American art, while not direct, is enormous." "Fine," she retorted, "so go there alone and give him

69

my regards." I glared at her and then, pretending to be hurt, went on, "To think that I'd kept that visit for the last so I could enjoy the simple charm of the Plaza Mayor with the bewitching flight of its black carrion crows overhead!" Although my words were pretentious, it produced the desired effect and she finally agreed, "Right, let's go."

'On our return across the dark but still scorching countryside of the Estremadura and Castela-a-Nova she asked, "In France is life going to be the same?" "What do you mean, life?" I asked, as though surprised. "This life we've spent without stopping, without resting, without sleeping, particularly without sleeping?" "France," I replied carefully, but in a way that wouldn't leave her in any doubt, "is as rich in architecture as Spain. I've come on this trip to do research and that's what I've got to do." This conversation was taking place at four in the morning and all she said was, "Fine; and what time are we leaving?" "Late, at about eleven, as the car has to have an oil change." "Great," she said, "that'll give me time to buy some things I need." The following morning she told me, "As you're going one way and I'm going the other, you'd better go now." "Right, but I want you here at eleven." "OK."

'When I got back at eleven and was about to go upstairs to our room the porter gave me a letter with a mocking irony coming from his tight lips, "From the lady." I calmly opened it. The letter read:

> *Luís*
>
> *I'm leaving for Portugal on the ten o'clock train, I'm fed up with cathedrals, and while it's hard to admit it, I'm also getting fed up with you. Above all I need to sleep. Over the last fortnight I've got covered in wrinkles and aged ten years and I'm not going to take any more. I have got one benefit from this trip – I've got to know you. I'm not the right woman for you, and you're not the right man for me. You don't like anything or anyone unless it's landscapes and stone. Me, I reckon I'm worth more than a view from the Tibidabo or the sight of the portico of Burgos Cathedral. Don't be cross with me. Goodbye.*
> *Antonieta*

'I felt slightly anxious, because I hadn't expected such rapid success, but at the same time there was an immense feeling of relief. The trip to France no longer interested me and the fact was that I, too, needed to sleep.'

'Look,' I said to the porter, I'm not going to have lunch. Just send someone to wake me at nine tonight.'

In the silence of the starry night Pedro's voice rose – a voice that shook with righteous indignation.

'I'm a very good friend of yours, Luís, but I have to tell you that I feel your behaviour demonstrates a treacherous hypocrisy.'

'You're quite wrong, Pedro, What it shows, in spite of appearances, is a deep humanity. So much so that...'

'So much so that?'

'That even now Antonieta and I still have tea together.'

'So you started seeing her again?'

'Of course. After a neurotic interlude there was no reason for us not to remain friends, since she still had her feelings and her woman's pride. And do you know what she asked me when we saw each other for the first time two years later?'

'I haven't got the least idea.'

'Just this. "Luís, tell me the truth. Did I make you suffer a lot? Did I? And have you forgiven me?"'

'And you didn't admit to what you'd done?'

'Good God no! All I did was make a gesture that covered everything, from floods of tears to dark thoughts of suicide. "Terribly, but one must go on, one must go on." "Am I forgiven?" she begged. "Completely, Antonieta." In a way of consolation, and perhaps as a confession, she went on to say, ' "Look Luís, men who let women sleep aren't nearly as worthwhile as men who don't let them sleep..."'

Pedro stood up in silence, and with a dry, 'See you some time,' walked into the night, bearing his broken heart and his disapproval.

Purity

Abílio Ramos looked at the sky with that dissatisfaction of a man who has not entirely achieved his desires. The stars shone dimly, their brightness diminished by the utilitarian light of the street lamps. The traffic had died down, but the sound of engines was still adding rhythm to the city in a slower, though no less intrusive and aggressive cadence. He looked up again and thought, 'It's a cloistered sky, a sky of imprisoned stars...' He suddenly had a desire for silence, for solitude and the empty skylines of the countryside.

The scent of the mulberry trees gradually began to spread and a ridiculous longing rose from the depths of his past, calling to mind the Praça da Vitória where he had been born.

'I'm nothing more than a failed man from the countryside,' he decided. Abílio Ramos was a man who had a constant need for classification. Throughout his entire life he had searched for formulae, never suspecting that words might be deceptive, starting from the premise of ideas for life rather than from life producing ideas.

The description of a 'failed man from the country' that he had applied to himself pleased him instantly.

He began to walk faster, as though he had lightened the burden that was weighing on his shoulders. Without admitting to it, he was happy in himself. He looked at the clock.

'It's time,' he murmured. 'She must be there by now.'

This time, unusually for him, he had left little to luck and knew that he would be able to carry on in his mental adventure, to proceed with it to the end. The formula he had worked out, which had become so attractive to him, had long been in need of proof. And now Fate had handed him so generously and unexpectedly the means of achieving it.

She was indeed there.

He went in as he usually did, looking distracted and pretending not to see her as he leaned on the counter.

'Give me a whisky.'

It was a little café that had a variety of customers: people coming in from work, local residents going home from shows, dubious types who would either speak loudly in order to attract attention or who would scheme in whispers, leaning over their tables, their heads together and their lips secretly planning a petty crime.

'It's nice weather, sir!'

'That's right, Sr Rogério. Spring has come.'

'I tell you sir that if I ruled the heavens I wouldn't allow anything except Spring. Well,' he went on as though making a concession to the All-Powerful, 'maybe a little bit of Autumn, because of the fruit. As for Summer and Winter, never! I don't like extremes or excesses.'

'Perhaps you're right, Sr Rogério, perhaps you're right. But just think, Winter...'

'Yes, Winter.'

And the conversation continued between the two in that neutral, trivial way of people who have nothing to say to each other and who believe that this is the only way they will get on.

As he was speaking, Abílio Ramos could feel her eyes fixed on the back of his neck. He guessed the silent eagerness with which she waited for him to turn round as she sat at the table at the other end of the café, sipping at a glass of milk.

He knew that she was alone, completely alone, and that she had turned everyone away, even though this would be damaging to her *business*, in order to conform to the idea he had formed of her – *that she thought he had formed of her.*

It had started some months earlier, just as, so often, the most important things in life start, with a little incident that seemed of no significance. As he was leaving a cake shop he had bumped into her and apologized politely.

'Do forgive me, madam.'

'It really doesn't matter at all.'

From then on he had greeted her with his customary politeness,

73

although not attaching any meaning to it. It was only much later that he had realized what this, and he, meant to her.

As he liked to walk the small streets at night he had known her for some time. Indeed there was more to it – he knew of her 'profession'. It was on a rainy night that she had approached him, and he had at once stared at the pale, regular face with its black twisted braids on either side and the deep-set eyes that still retained fragments of a squandered purity. From the tone of her voice and the shyness with which she spoke, he had recognized in her the unfulfilled vocation of the courtesan. Faced with his refusal, she had walked away untroubled, without looking him in the face, her small bag hanging down, her body swinging lightly in the usual, almost official manner of the paid provider of caresses.

He had not thought of it again. But now fate had brought her back into his life, or rather into the life of his mind, as though that small, insignificant incident of their bumping into each other had suddenly assumed a magic, transcendent importance.

He had seen her again a few days later arguing vehemently with a man in the street. His presence made her quieten down and she had quickly run off down the street, abandoning her companion in order to hide in a dark doorway, where she had remained watching him.

It was this which had caught his attention for the first time.

'The woman's frightened of me', he thought. Does she think I'm a policeman?' But he immediately discounted the idea. 'No, no one would take me for a policeman. It's obviously something else. Yes, it's something else.'

And suddenly the truth had spontaneously come to him in all its simplicity. 'She thinks I don't know what she is. She wants to be what she thinks I believe her to be. What if I were to make her be what she thinks I believe her to be?'

Abílio Ramos believed in Fate; not bodyless, faceless fate, but that intractable Fate of the Greeks which is implanted in human acts.

For him humans were split into the circumstantial and the essential, and he truly believed that he belonged to the latter, without realizing that there was a presumptuous vanity in such a conviction.

An essential being was one who intervened in Fate, by collaborating with it, by defying it, or by guiding it towards its true intentions.

However, one sole truth is simple in its apparent revelation and this truth was full of implications and consequences.

Once unleashed, his thoughts became more and more embedded in this entangled confusion.

He would repeat to himself, 'For her I am her fleeting hope. Only I, the man who walks down the road and whose name she doesn't even know, can give her self-respect, return her to her past purity. What I am, when all is said and done, is her last hope, the only thing that remains to her.'

From this, an as yet unformulated and imprecise notion of duty began to grow in him like a fermenting, transcendent affliction waiting to rise.

However, Abílio Ramos was incapable of intervening without first conceptualizing. All his actions were deductively thought through, starting from a principle which had of necessity to have been conceived earlier in order that the experience that resulted in denial or confirmation would acquire concrete expression. So that life should take on some reality he needed to prove it to himself and this proof could only be achieved through a pattern and a formula.

The notion of a duty to be fulfilled was not sufficient: it was vital that a concept justify the need for intervention in his mind.

It was at this precise moment that his old formula surfaced with the already definitive words, 'Yes, that's what it was. There was no doubt, that's what it was.'

And so in order to give it full expression, a reality that he might call material, he repeated out loud, 'It is necessary to pretend that people are good in order to make them better.'

And he repeated this over and over, not in order to ensure it would sink in, but so that he could absorb himself in the inherent force that irradiated from her.

'It is necessary to pretend that people are good in order to make them better.'

He had made up his mind. Now, through this woman, and with her unconscious help, he would have the uncontestable proof of this imagined truth.

He had no doubt as to his success. Armed with the force of a principle, he, Abílio Ramos, was going to transform a Venus of the streets, a poor degraded slut into a decent woman. Yes. He, Abílio Ramos, was going to return her to her true standing, to turn her fate onto the true path. So, without hesitating for a moment, he drew up a programme which he was prepared to stick to, to the last, minutest detail.

§

The woman's eyes remained fixed on him and Abílio Ramos turned slowly.

Slowly, like someone overcoming a long hesitation, while at the same time driven by an irresistible impulse, he walked towards her table.

'May I?'

'Of course.' And she blushed as she replied, as though not used to dealing with men.

'I apologize for my cheek, but the place is full and there's no other table.'

'Please don't worry.' From the outset she had thought that he was going to behave like the other men and make some coarse suggestion, which would shatter her dream. But his behaviour had reassured her.

He sensed her discomfort and went on:

'I know it's not very polite to sit at a lady's table when I haven't been introduced to her, but we're not complete strangers, are we?'

'No, we're not', she replied, delighted. 'We know each other very well by sight.'

'Good. I see you here almost every night at this time.'

'I come from the Company' she rushed to explain. 'I'm a telephonist and I work the first night shift.'

'I thought it must be that', he said, pretending to be convinced. Then he introduced himself.

'Abílio Ramos, lawyer.'

'Esmeralda Rodrigues', she replied simply.

'May I offer you some cakes.'

'Good heavens, don't trouble yourself.'

He had already called the waiter.

'Bring me a selection of cakes – good ones.'

'Yes, sir.'

In order to encourage her, he ate one.

'Do help yourself.'

She timidly took a cake and began to nibble at it, concealing her hunger.

'This woman's hungry,' Abílio Ramos thought to himself, and he pressed her:

'Go on, have another.'

She made a sign of refusal.

'Don't tell me you're not greedy. A woman has a duty to be greedy.'

'Do you think so?' she asked. She took another cake.

'Of course I think so.'

The conversation continued along this line for some time until she stood up.

'If you'll excuse me, I'm off. And thank you very much.'

'Please don't mention it.'

'Well, see you again,' she said as she left.

'See you tomorrow,' he replied purposefully.

'See you tomorrow,' she repeated, thrilled.

§

After that Abílio Ramos would see her almost every day and sit at her table.

He carefully encouraged her to take him into her confidence, and it was he who suggested that she should tell him things, protecting her from being dangerously near the truth when it came to difficult parts.

No one knew better than he that her tale was untrue, although it did contain a certain amount of truth. Truth when she spoke of her childhood; truth when she spoke of her father, who adored her and who had died suddenly, leaving her destitute. And truth even when she spoke of what she could have been, as though she had been that.

Esmeralda had stayed at school until the fifth year and always, with rare exceptions, used modest language, so making the task easier for Abílio Ramos. As one knows, words hold much more importance for familiarity than ideas and so, when it came to important points, it was Abílio Ramos who, helped by them, managed to suggest what her reply should be.

In addition he knew that lying wasn't natural to her, but with his help, and without realizing it, she began to construct the fragile fabric of her imagined life.

'I understand,' he would say, 'what your life must have been like after your father's death. A little girl all alone, in a world full of traps and temptations, needs a lot of courage. But you're a brave woman.'

'Not as much as you think, sir.'

'Oh yes, more than you think,' he insisted.

One night at the beginning of summer he asked suddenly, 'When is your day off?'

She hesitated a moment without knowing what to say and then picked at random, 'Saturday. Yes, Saturday. I only go back to work on Sunday afternoon.'

'Perfect,' he said. 'That's a good day for me too. So listen, Esmeralda,' (he had begun to call her affectionately by her name), 'would you take it badly if I invited you to spend Saturday with me at a little beach near Lisbon?' And, without waiting for a reply, he added, as though wanting to overcome a resistance he had already foreseen, 'It's a quiet little beach where hardly anyone goes. Wild, but beautiful.'

She sat speechless, looking at him, thrilled and at the same time confused.

'Look,' said Abílio Ramos, pretending to think that he had offended her with his invitation, 'I know that there are ladies who don't like to go alone with a man who's not related to them. If that's the problem, I wouldn't be upset.'

'Not at all. I'm very grateful to you and shall come with you with pleasure.'

'Where shall I pick you up? At your house?'

She hesitated again.

'No, perhaps not at my house.'

'I understand,' he said. 'Because of the neighbours, yes? I do understand.'

'Yes,' she replied faintly.

'So here? At nine, OK?'

'OK. At nine.'

§

It was a marvellous morning the next day. The beach was isolated, just as Abílio Ramos had said it would be, and was protected by two very high, rocky cliffs which appeared to capture the blue of the sky. The sea swept, restrained, onto the beach in constant white, foam waves.

'It's beautiful, isn't it?' Esmeralda exclaimed. 'So beautiful and pure, don't you think?'

'I do,' Abílio Ramos replied. 'It looks like a sea that belongs to the beginning of the world.'

He gave her his arm and they wandered the entire morning, hardly speaking, she wrapped in her dream and he proud of his work. However, something was missing, a sort of real proof which he did not yet dare assume. Although he tried to hide it from himself, he felt that there was something wholly dishonest in his behaviour, but the unrelenting need for confirmation of his principles was becoming an irresistible temptation.

'You know, Esmeralda,' he said after they had eaten lunch in a small restaurant built at the top of the rocks, 'I've been thinking about something.'

'What? Tell me.'

'I don't know if I ought to. I don't know whether you'll take it the wrong way.'

'I wouldn't take anything the wrong way.'

'Well, here goes: how old are you?'

'Twenty-nine,' she replied, astonished. 'Why?'

'Why?' Now it was his turn to feel embarrassed. He had the feeling that there was something hypocritical and cowardly in his behaviour and he hesitated for a moment. 'Because at twenty-nine it's time for you to think about changing your position.'

'Changing my position? I don't understand.'

'Thinking about marrying.'

'Marrying?' she asked, astonished. 'I've never thought about it. Anyway, who would want to marry me?'

'That's silly!' He knew that he wasn't risking anything and that, if his theory was correct, she would say no. 'That's silly. Me, for instance.'

'You!' Her face contorted in fear. 'You! A man like you marry me!'

'So what's wrong with that?'

'Me? A woman like me?'

'Like you? What do you mean?'

By now she was pale and trembling and could only speak hesitantly.

'What do I mean? You, a man of your position, marrying a woman like me? A simple telephonist?'

'There's only one reason for you to refuse,' he said implacably.
'That's that you don't like me. That's it, you don't like me, do you?'

She looked into his eyes.

'I do. I like you more than anyone in the world. I do, but I don't
want – I can't marry you. And I beg of you, I beg of you', her voice became pleading and sad like a small child's, 'I beg of you not to talk about
it again. Do you promise?'

'If that's what you want, I promise.'

'Thank you.'

She began to sob convulsively.

'Don't cry,' he begged. 'I shan't talk about it any more.' He put his
arm round her waist and began to wipe her eyes with a handkerchief.
'Don't cry. Come on, it's late.'

He felt moved, not by her tears but with the proud feeling of someone who has completed a dreamed-of task.

'Now she's redeemed,' he thought to himself. 'Now she's pure
again! Pure as though she'd been born this minute! I was right. *You have
to believe that people are good in order for them to become better.* I was right.

§

Abílio Ramos picked up the letter unhurriedly. It was written on
cheap paper in a hesitant hand that he did not recognize. As usual, he
was about to put it in his pocket to read quietly in the office, but something made him change his mind, something indefinable that struck
him about the sloping writing, the short *t*, the lack of dots on the *i*. He
sensed a feeling of dejection and helplessness as he looked at the envelope, a sort of despair.

He was already on the landing when he decided to go back so that,
methodical as ever, he could open the envelope with a paper knife.

He read the letter once and then again, nervously, with the sheet
of paper trembling in his hand, his eyes half-closed as though he were
weakly refusing to take in its meaning. It read:

Sir

Yesterday was the happiest and the saddest day of my life. I owe the happiness to you and the sadness entirely to me and my miserable condition. Because of my happiness and my sadness I couldn't sleep.

Now I feel that I can no longer go on lying to you and misleading you.

I'm not what you think. I'm not a serious girl worthy of your respect and kindness. I'm a woman of easy virtue, a woman whose life only deserves disgust.

However, that isn't really true either. I'm not a woman of easy virtue now. After I met you, after you treated me so kindly, I did everything I could to be what you thought I was. God knows how many sacrifices I made for that. But when you sink so low it's very hard to get back up. Everything pulls you back down. I wanted to work, but I didn't know how to work any more, and when I did get work it didn't take long for people to find out who I was – or who I had been – and they'd sack me.

It's like leprosy, and there isn't a cure for leprosy.

But that isn't what's troubling me. The hungrier I got and the more sacrifices I made, nothing would pay for what you have unknowingly done for me. And that's what I want to say to you, so that you keep it in mind.

I'm not a lost woman, sir. With your kindness you saved me from this curse. I beg of you, believe me – do believe me. Now I feel as pure – more pure – than before the terrible decision that led me to this. Believe me. The reason I'm like this I owe entirely to you. But that's how I feel, and not how others feel. For other people I'll always be the woman I was, the woman who belonged to everyone. And now I'll be the same thing for you, because this is a stain that is only washed away inside, and souls can't be seen.

I wanted to deceive myself, but yesterday when you took me out to lunch and for a walk on the beach, treating me like a lady, I became sure that I was lost for ever. There was one of the many men I've known at the table next to us, and when he saw us he said to his companion, 'Look, look. That tart has found herself a hanger-on.' Fortunately you didn't hear, but I did, and it was enough.

I realised at that moment that I was an embarrassment to you, an embarrassment to the person I loved most and to whom I owed my salvation. So then I thought that I mustn't see you any more, but I also felt that I couldn't stop seeing you.

So this evening I came to the conclusion that my problem has no cure.

And so I'm saying goodbye to you, sir, goodbye for ever.

May God bless you and forgive me.

Esmeralda

A terrible anxiety took hold of Abílio Ramos. He ran downstairs. An ambulance was going by at breakneck speed, its siren screaming. Abílio Ramos, although not superstitious, saw this as a bad omen. He tried to calm himself, but was unable to. 'Pull yourself together,' he thought, 'it's nothing. Absolutely nothing. Why am I preparing myself for a tragedy?' But his heart continued to beat rapidly and he hailed a taxi. Although she had never told him, he knew where she lived, as he had followed her one night. It was a narrow little street in a poor district, the paint peeling off the houses with their steep, crumbling steps. He ran up the stairs two at a time and on the third floor knocked on the door.

An old woman opened it. Her hair was wispy and dirty and her small, lively, piercing eyes stood out from her wrinkled face like an anomaly.

'Miss Esmeralda?' he asked, trying to appear calm.

'Miss Esmeralda?' She opened her toothless mouth. 'God help me... She's gone.'

'Doesn't she live here?'

'Yes, she does and she doesn't.'

'I don't understand,' said Abílio Ramos. 'Explain, for God's sake!'

'Are you her man?' the old woman asked, apparently wanting to find things out before answering.

'No, just a friend.'

'A friend. Ah!' the old woman exclaimed in surprise. 'I didn't know she had friends. Come in, please.' And she stood aside so that he could enter.

Abílio Ramos went in and the old woman shut the door.

'I don't like to give people reason to talk.' And she went on to explain, 'The neighbours don't have anything to do with me. That suits me fine.'

Now it was the old woman who was asking the questions. Abílio Ramos curbed his impatience.

'So you were a friend of hers? You're telling me she had friends? Great friends they were to let her come to this.'

'To what? For God's sake, senhora...'

'Engrácia, at your service.'

'Senhora Engrácia, tell me, what's happened?'

'I'm coming to that, I'm coming to that. Give me time. There's no hurry, as you won't be able to do any good.'

Abílio Ramos became still more anxious but he realised that the old woman was stubborn and wouldn't tell him anything without having her say. He fell into a chair, disheartened.

'Excuse me...'

'Please do. Make yourself at home.'

He looked around him. It was a simple but clean room where the old woman's grubbiness stood out like a stain.

'Friends, you're telling me?' she repeated. 'I knew that she had men. And because she was a nice girl I even let her have some of them in the house. The neighbours did complain once, but it didn't make any difference. Friends! For some time now she hasn't brought any men here. And it wasn't their fault, as they still wanted her. But she didn't want them. I don't know what came upon her. So her life went from bad to worse, and I fell on bad times too. She owed me three lots of rent.'

'I'll pay the outstanding rent,' said Abílio Ramos, taking the initiative. He began to pull out his wallet.

'Thank you,' the old woman broke in. 'I don't want it. I'm poor, but I've also got my pride. I helped her out and that should mean my sins aren't all counted. And I'm not going to be able to do anything else for her, poor thing. If you'd wanted to pay her rent you should have paid earlier, and then perhaps she wouldn't have done what she did.'

'But what did she do?'

'What can one of God's poor children do when she doesn't have any work or money for food and has a bed given her out of charity? She did what she had to do... She did what she thought was right – and, God forgive me – what I thought was right.'

'But what?' Abilío Ramos asked, desperately impatient.

'This morning,' said Senhora Engrácia solemnly, 'I knocked on her bedroom door as usual to take her a coffee and a roll. (Just because she didn't pay me was no reason for her to go hungry. She might go hungry elsewhere but not when I'm around.) I knocked and knocked but she didn't answer. If she'd been like she used to be I wouldn't have worried. Lots of nights she stayed out, but recently she always came home. Late, but she'd come home. "Miss Esmeralda!" I called. "Miss Esmeralda!" Nothing. I pushed at the door, which was closed and pushed again and, because she hadn't put the chain across it was easy to open. "Miss Esmeralda." I opened the window and saw her. There she lay. She was dressed... dressed and just how! Just think how! As a bride; that's right, as a bride.'

'Was she dead?'

'No; if only she were. She was alive, but showing no sign of life. I called and called her but she didn't reply and I couldn't take my eyes off her, I was terrified. She was beautiful, sir. So beautiful; I'd never seen a bride so beautiful. It's wrong to say it but she looked like a picture of Our Lady, may God forgive me. "Now there's a thing," I thought, "where did the poor creature get the money?" I only realized when she was taken away and I saw the empty wardrobe. She had sold or pawned everything: her dresses, her shoes, her handbag and I'm sure she even sold the gold medal with the picture of her father that she never went anywhere without! This note was next to her.'

The old woman rummaged in the pocket of the patched dressing gown she was wearing and read out slowly:

> *Senhora Engrácia*
> *Forgive me for the trouble I'm causing you but I can't go on with this life. Thank you for everything you've done for me and for the favour I'm about to ask. I want to be buried like this. The money for the burial is in my bedside table.*
> *Goodbye*
> *Esmeralda*

'And it was. If it had been anyone else they'd have taken the rent from it but I'm not like that. So I gave it to the firemen who took her away, just as she'd left it.'

Abílio Ramos stood up suddenly and took the note from her.

'Where have they taken her?'

'To the hospital.'

Abílio Ramos was concerned, and rapidly summed up the situation. 'She must have gone to the emergency department.'

'Thank you for the trouble you've taken,' Abílio Ramos said to her.

'There's nothing to thank me for, but there is something I'd like to say: men are the pits: they bring women to this and it's only later that they feel any shame.'

Abílio Ramos could no longer hear her as he ran down the stairs.

***

The surgeon on duty – an old colleague from high school – asked for the list of admittances.

'No, there's no one here of that name. She came in this morning, you say?'

'Yes, but perhaps she went to another hospital.'

'Not possible,' the other replied. 'In the state you say she was in she would only have come here. Can't you give me any more information?'

Abílio Ramos hesitated for a moment. A sort of modesty had left him tongue-tied.

'A girl... in a bridal gown.'

'Your fiancée?'

'Oh no!' And he went on decisively, 'On the other hand, who knows? Perhaps she was my fiancée.'

The surgeon looked at him, confused.

'That's great! Call the sister,' he told a cleaner who was going past.

'Was a woman admitted in a bad state in a bridal gown?' he asked the nurse.

'Yes, Doctor. I have to say we laughed.'

'Why did you laugh? I can't see any reason for that,' the surgeon remarked tartly.

'It's just that,' the nurse apologized, 'a prostitute dressed as a bride is a bit out of place.'

'We can all dress as we like. So was she called Esmeralda?'

'No, Doctor. She's called Leonor... Leonor what? Leonor Rodrigues.'

'Her working name,' the surgeon remarked. 'And why didn't you tell me about her?'

'It's not a surgical matter and you were asleep.'

'So how is she? Is there any hope?'

'I don't think so, Doctor. It was two packs of Phenobarbital. At about midday she did seem to be getting better and she asked for a crucifix. But she's slipped back now. We've done all we could.'

'I do know. Off you go, Sister.'

The two were alone again.

'Zé,' Abílio Ramos said, almost pleading. 'I want you to do me a favour. Let me see her.'

'It's against regulations and it'll only upset you. She's in the emergency ward.'

'I don't care. Just do that for me.'

The surgeon looked at him steadily.

'Right, let's go. Pretend that you're a doctor.'

Her bed was hidden from the rest of the ward by a screen. Serum was running drip by drip from a flask that was connected to her arm by a rubber tube. Abílio Ramos looked at her. Her breathing was irregular and rasping, her mouth open, her eyes closed and her face was slightly twisted. Her livid hands were resting on the dark blanket.

Abílio Ramos took hold of one of her hands.

'Esmeralda, it's me,' he said. 'Can you hear me? Tell me that you can hear me.'

Her fingers stiffened and lightly squeezed his hand.

'Can you hear me? It's me here next to you. Me.'

Esmeralda opened her eyes and her mouth moved as though she wanted to speak, but the words were unclear.

'Don't try to speak, don't try to speak,' Abílio Ramos went on. 'I'm here. I'll always be near you. But you've got to live. Can you hear me? You've got to live!' he begged.

She made an enormous effort and murmured almost inaudibly, 'It's late, but I'm happy... I'm happy. Thank you!'

She had a convulsion and breathed heavily. Then she became still. Her open eyes remained staring at him and had taken on a strange gentleness. Her face had become supernaturally calm. The hands that had for a moment clutched at the folds of the bedcover had stretched out. A sense of the unreal and of purity emanated from her and Abílio

Ramos knelt down. His despair took hold of him suddenly and welled up in him. His entire body shook.

He walked unsteadily towards the surgeon, who was checking on a patient at the other side of the ward.

'Zé,' he asked. 'Come over here. She's not well.'

The surgeon turned, looked at her for a moment and said, 'No, she's not well.' He leaned over her, felt her pulse, listened to her for a moment and said coldly, 'Rather, she's better than ever – she's dead.' He looked at her again and, suddenly moved, added, 'What an extraordinary face for such a woman! She looks like a virgin.'

'Dead? Are you sure she's dead?' Abílio Ramos asked.

'Absolutely.'

It was only then that Abílio Ramos took in what was being said. His face was ashen and his eyes full of tears.

'What's the matter?'

'Nothing.'

'Come on.'

'Let me stay here a while.'

'You can't.'

Abílio Ramos quickly leaned towards her and kissed her forehead. The surgeon pulled him out of the ward.

'What the hell is this all about?' he asked. 'Knowing you as I do I confess I'm astonished. I never thought you were capable of this. Listen, were you in love with her?'

'No,' he replied gravely.

'Sorry – was she related to you?'

'Not that, either.'

'Friends?'

'Not even that.'

'Well then I don't understand your behaviour, and I don't understand your problem either.'

'It's just that...' Abílio Ramos replied. 'It's just that... I killed her. *That's right. I killed her.*'

The surgeon looked at him in astonishment.

'What? You killed her? You're out of your mind.'

'Yes, I know. And yes, I killed her. Not the way you or anyone else might think. I didn't give her poison and I didn't suggest suicide to her. Not that. I just tried to change her, to purify her. And unfortunately I succeeded. But this is how I succeeded – by killing her! I was just per-forming an experiment – pretending to believe that she wasn't what she was, so that she would stop being that. Do you understand?'

'Not really, but anyway...'

'And it was the experiment that killed her...'

'Well you do at least have to be forgiven for not predicting the result.'

'That's true, but it's not enough. And I shan't be blamed for it, but my conscience will blame me. The fact is that it was my theory that killed her.'

'If that's all,' the surgeon responded a little cynically, 'I don't think you should trouble yourself, as it's not exactly original. Thousands of people die, even millions, in every generation, because of the theories of others.'

A nurse went to call the surgeon for an operation.

'Sorry, Abílio, I've got to go. Just resign yourself.'

'Don't worry about me. Thanks for everything. I've got to go too.'

When Abílio Ramos left the hospital the evening light was bathing the castle's battlements with a pink haze. He walked down the narrow street and joined the other pedestrians. There, amongst others, he felt protected from himself.

'I killed her,' he thought to himself. 'I killed her. The fact is that I crossed the frontiers of the inevitable, from which no one can return. I killed the most pure woman I've ever known. Perhaps the only really pure woman I've ever known. I'm a monster! An intellectual monster, but I'm a monster.'

He turned a corner at random and walked down a dark street. Without realizing what he was doing, he was gesticulating and talking to himself. A woman stopped, astonished, as she watched him. He came to himself and stood in front of her.

'Listen, tell me, do you think I have the face of an assassin? You don't think so? Well I am.'

The woman fled in horror.

'The man's mad...'

'So there,' he thought, 'do you have to pretend that people are good in order to make them better? What a fool! A fine recipe for killing people.'

Suddenly an idea came to him like a blinding light. 'Great fool. I should have done the opposite. No, no. That truth is something else. What you have to do is *show people that you know them and accept them for what they are.* That's the only thing that's humane and honourable. That's the only thing that can save them.'

And he repeated out loud, '*What you have to do is show people that you know them and accept them for what they are.*'

Abílio Ramos had discovered a formula and the more he repeated it the more his distress and remorse receded, as though something greater than he and his conscience had arrived to restore his calm and self-respect.

The Day of Reckoning

Dr Silvano carefully wiped his thick-lensed spectacles, put them on the windowsill and looked at us with his round, myopic, lacklustre eyes.

We all knew that, for him, we were now merely smoky shadows, an almost bodyless audience. We also knew that Dr Silvano was about to speak, but that because of his shyness when he was lecturing he couldn't cope with the clear, vivid sight of people or things.

For more than an hour he had listened to our discussion on life and death and had waited until we had run out of anything else to say on the subject, so that he could give us what he believed to be the last word. This was his one and only vanity, but such a vanity that we had come to the conclusion that he only spoke to himself, like someone wanting to confirm externally an interior certainty.

'There are few people,' he began, 'who have lived with death as much as I. Of course death is present in every act of life: in love, in fame, in success and lack of success, like an unavoidable shadow. And the strangest thing is that it is precisely in sickness that it agrees to a fight, even if transitory, in which it may win or lose. On this point, good health is much more dangerous than illness and so I agree with the wise Professor Richet, who would always begin his lectures with the words, 'Good health, my esteemed students, is a transitory state that never augurs well...'

We laughed discreetly and, when silence was resumed, Dr Silvano went on, 'Besides this, death is much maligned and frequently doesn't possess the implacable character attributed to it. In this respect, life is

90

far more implacable and demanding than death because it always sets the performance of certain acts as a condition. I know that no one wants to die, not even those who kill themselves, because suicide is the precipitate act of someone fed up with life. I also know that men go to all lengths to survive... To all lengths, from the gods to worldly fame, which is not as ephemeral as it might seem. I don't mean to suggest that life is eternal – I don't know, and I'm not concerned about that – but I do say that, through their results, acts in life *are* eternal, because they will have indeterminate repercussions until the end of time...

'But let's get on. I said that death isn't as implacable as it seems, and I can vouch for this because I have watched it grant strange favours and inexplicably respect certain contracts and promises.'

Dr Silvano fell silent in order to enjoy the effect of his words and we remained waiting for the story that would inevitably justify this enigma.

'A long time ago,' he went on, stressing his words, 'when Lisbon was not yet the jostling, noisy city we know today, I was doctor to a mother and son in Trás-os-Montes. They were 'new Christians', descendants of Jews who had converted many centuries ago but whose racial characteristics had not diminished in any way. These were as obvious, both in their appearance and in their actions, as though they had remained practising Jews. I don't want you to think that my use of the words 'Jews' is in any way pejorative. Quite the opposite, as if there's a maligned race it is theirs. It was not they who invented the instruments of usury because, as you well know, we owe coinage to the Assyrians and notes of exchange and loans to the Phoenicians and the Greeks. For that reason I am unable to understand the persecution to which they have been victim since time immemorial.

'Being generous, idealistic and devout, they understood that life was an exchange of services and through their intelligence they never make a contract without negotiation, particularly when material benefits are at stake. However, they do this less through greed than through a sense of justice and equilibrium. This is very much one of their characteristics.

'I was present at just such a contract – I was there as was Death, which was to act inevitably as the needle on the scales. It was also on this occasion that I saw Death accede and wait, simply in order to respect a strange covenant.

'As I have said, the family comprised just the mother and son. The mother, Dona Sara, who was over ninety and her son, Sr Navarro, who was seventy something. Dona Sara was small and appeared weak, with slight, insignificant infirmities (the middle-class – particularly the rich middle-class – consider it wrong not to be ill from time to time), but in fact she was as healthy as they come, which explained her active and re-markably long life. As for him, he had the constitution of an ox, but suf-fered from an obsession with illness – that obsession that doctors should never cure, since it represents a substantial part of their income...

'But good health is very dangerous, as I have already said – par-ticular in old age – and it is precisely because she enjoyed good health that, when she was trying to clean the top of a wardrobe, perched up a ladder, she fell and broke a leg.

'The old woman was tough and, contrary to what one might think, her leg was already mending when pulmonary stagnation set in resulting in that type of drawn-out broncho-pneumonia with no fever but which in those days, with the resources available, could rarely be cured, particularly in the elderly.

'It was the middle of October and the weather had turned damp and rainy, which also didn't help. One day, since things were going from bad to worse, I called a meeting with the most famous clinician of the time in order to share the responsibility and relieve my conscience.

'Unhappily for the old thing, the expert confirmed my pessimistic prognosis. "You've done everything you can and there's nothing more to do..." And he went on, "It's not as though she's dying young."

' "No, certainly not," I agreed. "She's ninety-seven..." And then I asked, "So, Professor, you are of the opinion that..."

' "That she's dying... That she'll die shortly." Then he added con-fidently, "Three or four days at maximum."

'That was my opinion, but because of my nature and as a matter of routine, I argued, "But look, Professor, she's still lucid and talking..."

' "That doesn't mean anything. There are people who speak up to the end." And he went on sardonically, "Famous people, for instance, always have some phrase to hand down to posterity..."

'So there was nothing else to do but tell her son, and although it is always upsetting to have to give this sort of news to a member of the fam-ily, in fact it didn't overly concern me since Sr Navarro seemed to have known for some time what was going on. Indeed, since the broncho-pneumonia had appeared and I had kept him up-to-date with the situation, Sr Navarro appeared, at least, to be resigned. He therefore had never asked whether she could be cured or not, but simply how long she could last, or "hang on", as he put it.

' "Could she hang on for three or four months, doctor?"

'At that stage things had not reached the acute dramatic aspect that now appeared and I had conceded, "Three or four months – maybe... Yes, your mother is tough and her heart is strong... Perhaps..."

'However, the situation had changed more rapidly than I had imagined and the opinion of the specialist weighed on my mind. I therefore decided to speak bluntly to him. "Sr Navarro," I told him solemnly as he walked with me to the hallway, "I have something to tell you. Your mother..."

' "My mother?" he interrupted anxiously. "My mother...?"

' "Your mother is terminally ill..." And in order to avoid the question that he would most certainly pose, taking my courage in my hands I went on, "The longest she can live is three or four days."

'Sr Navarro stood there stunned. "Three or four days, doctor? Three or four days? That's impossible..."

"Unfortunately it's not... That's my opinion and – more importantly – it's the Professor's opinion."

'Suddenly Sr Navarro had the most extraordinary and unexpected reaction one could imagine. He raised his voice and spoke scathingly, "So what does the opinion of the Professor count for? I confess...", and he went on, shouting louder and louder, his voice now sounding furious, "I confess I never expected this of you... That's right, I never expected it of you..." And Sr Navarro looked at me, his eyes burning with hatred, as though the Professor and I were in a conspiracy to kill his mother. "Three or four days, you say?" Then he laughed harshly, "Ah ha, three or four days, that's it? Is that all? Look, doctor, this may be the case with anyone else's mother, but not mine, understand?"

'My initial reaction was one of irritation, but I soon realized that Sr Navarro was having an attack of nerves which, as a doctor, I had to take into consideration. Besides that, I had on several occasions observed that even when forewarned, people are rarely able to accept the idea of the death of a loved one. Indeed psychological understanding rarely goes along with rational understanding, and it is quite true that death is an inescapable reality that is hard to accept.

'My professional conscience overruled the fact of my being human and I felt it my duty to do everything possible to calm him down. He continued to look at me, his hands shaking and lips trembling. His voice was quieter and his words had become an unintelligible murmur.

' "Sr Navarro," I began gently, "we have all had a mother and we have all suffered when she died. For instance I was a boy, little more than an adolescent, when my mother passed away. She was still a young woman and I well remember how much it hurt. You, Sr Navarro, have had great happiness – that of living with your mother for a long time. Few can boast of reaching seventy and their mother still being alive. However, there is an end to everything in this world, because that's man's condition... So you must get used to it, like we all get used to it... If you believe in God, then you must believe that it's His will..."

'Sr Navarro was now looking at me with pleading eyes and I felt sure that my words had produced the desired effect.

' "Forgive me, doctor," he said quietly. "Forgive me. It's just that I wasn't expecting this." His voice was now so entreating that I began to fear he would kneel at my feet, and so I grabbed his arm. "Just, please, do everything so that she goes on living... Bring in all the specialists you want... Buy the most expensive medicines... Spend day and night here, as I'll make up for any losses and pay whatever you think necessary... I'm not asking for anything else – just that she should live at least three or four months more. Do you see? Three or four months!"

'This filial love filled me with respect and I was deeply moved, but my professional conscience didn't allow me to deceive him.

' "Sr Navarro," I said, firmly and comfortingly, "I should love to grant you your request, but I've done everything I can and know how. I'm not infallible, and although I don't believe that with the resources available anyone can do anything more, I wouldn't take it badly were you to call in another doctor. Indeed, call any doctors you wish."

' "Doctor," Sr Navarro replied, "I don't doubt your knowledge, but at the moment – forgive me – I doubt your understanding. Don't you see that my mother can't die in less than three months? What's the date today? 22nd October? What you fail to understand is that my mother cannot die before the 15th January."

'I looked at him, astonished. This was indeed beyond my comprehension.

' "And why the 15th January?" I asked in surprise.

'"Because," and at this point Sr Navarro spelled out his words, "because it's only on the 15th January that the title deeds for the land we have in Trás-os-Montes will be ready. Do you own property?"

' "No," I replied angrily. "No, fortunately not."

'Sr Navarro didn't notice the change in my attitude and explained volubly, "Then you know nothing about the problems landowners have, particularly those who have land in the district of Braganza, in Trás-os-Montes. Oh, doctor, for centuries, and up to a short time ago, buying and selling was done by word of mouth. People were men of their word and a deed of sale was almost an insult. My grandfather – my mother's father – bought most of his land that way. Now you should see the problems I've been through to put the matter straight. And if my mother dies before the deeds have been drawn up it'll be the end of everything for me. It's as though I were rich but didn't have anything to show for it. I've got her power of attorney, but it will be null and void at her death. And it's only on that date that everything will be ready. Now do you understand?"

'I was astounded. I understood. I understood all too well. What I had thought was filial love was nothing more than sordid greed dictated by the most repugnant self-interest.

'The pity I had felt had been transformed into a deep disgust, almost hatred, and I was astonished to find myself wanting his mother to die then and there, just so that I could maliciously enjoy the despair of this miser.

' "This is all very well, Sr Navarro," I told him drily and harshly, "but it's of no interest to me. I only think of the life and health of the people I'm treating and the outcome of their death doesn't concern me. Whether you come out of this rich or poor is your problem, not mine. What I can tell you" – and I spoke like a judge who is pronouncing a death sentence –"is that your mother has no more than three days to live... I've told you, and that's how it is."

'Sr Navarro had noticed my disgust and retorted angrily, "Do you think so? You think that? Are you prepared to take a bet that she'll live until the day I name? Will you take a bet? You doctors know a lot and are very clever, but you don't realize that matters of life and death also depend on us and our will. That's something you don't know how to deal with, but she will deal with it. Do you want to see? Come with me."

95

'I wanted to hit him, but something stronger than me made me follow him to his mother's room.

'The old woman was lying there dying at the end of the bed. It was a cloudy day and through the window a dull light would brighten and then die down, making a flickering shadow on the headboard, at one moment moving round her head and at another rising in a spiral, rather like gaseous smoke.

'Sr Navarro sat on the bed and leaned towards her.

' "Can you hear me, mother?" Dona Sara opened her eyes without replying. "Can you hear me?" The old woman's eyes brightened and she made a slight movement with her head to show that she understood. "Well, listen to me. Your doctor says that you're not going to live for more than three or four days. But that mustn't happen. You promised me you'd live until the deeds were drawn up and you know that if that's not done in time it will be your fault. You've always been a good mother and you're not going to go back on your word and ruin your son, are you mother?"

'This dialogue with a dying woman was both unbelievable and monstrous and my duty as a doctor was to interrupt it, but I felt that we weren't alone. That's right, that we weren't alone. I sensed that Death was there too, leaning over and listening carefully so that it could weigh up the arguments and reasons, in the impenetrable depths of its mystery, and then come to a decision. This sensation was so intense that there was a moment when I almost felt I could see death, waving its symbolic scythe not only above the old woman's head, but above our heads too. I had a shiver a fear...

' "Mother," Sr Navarro continued. "Mother, you've got to live until the 15th January. Do you hear me? Until the 15th January. Then it's up to you. I'm not asking for anything else."

'The old woman's lips trembled. I could see that she was making an enormous effort to speak.

' "My son," she said in a weak, almost inaudible voice, "my son, it's true that I promised... but I don't know if I can... Maybe the doctor's right."

' "You can't do this to me mother... You can't do this to me," Sr Navarro argued, both irritated and pleading. "Don't go ruining a life full of dedication at the hour of your death."

'Then he went on like someone presenting an irrefutable argument and a convincing reason: "Besides which, your serge dress is worn out and your shoes are old... And you can't go to the grave dressed like that..."

' "Of course I can't... Will you order new ones for me? Will you?"

'The desire to negotiate – a characteristic of her race – was obvious now and the old woman's eyes shone.

' "Promise?"

' "I promise... If you give me time to do it."

' "I'll do what I can, son."

'Suddenly a ray of sunlight came through the window and dissolved the shadows in the room. The sense of death's presence was no longer there and I had the immediate impression that I had just come out of a dark abyss. I left the room without saying a word, followed by Sr Navarro and, without shaking his hand, I opened the door at the top of the stairs and left.

§

'When I left it was my intention not to return. As far as I could see my appearance as a doctor was unnecessary and my relationship with Sr Navarro had, clearly, become difficult. But a stronger argument than my distaste altered my decision. There was now a timescale and a day of reckoning in the most absurd contract a person could have observed.

'I had been a sort of witness and my duty was therefore to carry on to the end. For that reason the following day I went there as usual and I must admit that Sr Navarro welcomed me with his customary friendly politeness, as though nothing had happened. The only allusion to it was, in a way, cheerful.

' "The bet still stands, doctor." He took my silence as approval and went on, "And you are going to lose."

'The situation was so extraordinary that his behaviour didn't surprise me at all.

'I confess that for the first three days my burning desire was that the old woman should die. What absolves me from this unkind thought was that she really wasn't living, but vegetating. I must also add in my favour that during those three days I redoubled my efforts with her, for what one thinks and desires is one thing while what one does is another... Strange though it may seem, I wanted to win the bet not in order to increase my personal importance, but in the spirit of justice – or what

97

I perceived to be justice. I wanted to see the avarice of that parasite punished and this, it seemed to me – and I must now confess my error – was as important and necessary as a human life.

'Three days went by. The old woman's pulse became weaker and weaker and one could hardly hear her heart. When I arrived on the fourth day I was quite certain that it would all be over. But no. Without any sign of irony in his voice, before I could ask a question, Sr Navarro told me, "She's just the same. And a while ago she asked what time you were coming..."

'I went into her room and looked at her and, for the first time, saw in the face of the dying woman a determination that astounded me. It was only then that I understood. For the love of her son, through pride and even through a contractual obligation, the woman wanted to keep her promise against all the odds, against physiology, against pathology and, if possible, even against Fate and the will of God.

'I'm very sensitive to noble behaviour and from that moment, for very different reasons from those of Sr Navarro, I began to want her to live until the named day. When I was leaving I turned to shake Sr Navarro's hand and, moved, I told him with sincerity, "It looks as though I've lost the bet... and let's hope so! I hope so from the bottom of my heart..."

' "Thank you, doctor."

'The 15th January came. The evening before she had had a cardiac arrest but, against all odds, she had recovered and I confess that when I rang the bell my heart was beating rapidly. It was not that I was in any doubt – for mysterious reasons death had stuck to that absurd agreement and had agreed to it and I was sure that death would carry through its concession to the end.

' "Still alive?" I asked, without any greeting.

' "Still alive," Sr Navarro replied. "And look, doctor, look."

'Sr Navarro was eagerly clutching two bundles of notarized paper in his hands.

' "Look, doctor. Everything, everything's ready. Nothing's missing – the transfers of ownership, the deeds and the certificates. Everything!" His jubilant voice shook in manic euphoria. "Everything." But suddenly, as though coming to himself, he added rather sadly, "Come and see her doctor, come."

'I followed him. The pale January sun lit the room. I looked at

Dona Sara. She was lying on her back clutching the new serge dress against her breast and from each of her crossed hands hung a black shoe.

'I bent over to examine her, but Sr Navarro told me not to. "Don't take them from her, doctor. Don't take them," he pleaded. "She was so happy."

'I straightened up and murmured, "It really makes no difference."

'A cloud hid the sun and once again I had the sensation of the presence of death. Not that death that makes concessions, but implacable death, the enemy of life.

' "It makes no difference."

'I went on watching her and suddenly saw the dress slip and the shoes fall from her hands...

' "She's dead," I murmured. I quickly listened to her and confirmed, "She's just died."

'Sr Navarro fell to his knees and began to sob, "Poor thing, poor thing! Doctor," he asked in a hesitating voice, "do me a favour and call the maid."

'I went to call her and when she entered he simply said, "Conceição, come and help me. I want to dress her and put on her shoes. She wanted to go to the grave looking beautiful and that's how she'll go." And he went on, "Doctor, send me your bill, and double it, as you deserve it."

'I didn't reply. I turned and quickly went downstairs.'

§

Dr Silvano fell silent and waited for our comments.

'Very interesting,' we said in chorus. 'But what does it prove in the end?' one of the braver members of our group asked.

Dr Silvano was speechless for a moment, but only hesitated for a short while.

'What does it prove?' he asked sternly. 'It proves nothing. Neither life nor death is a theorem that can be demonstrated... However, there is one conclusion that can be drawn, which is that the will of men doesn't stand still when one is at the limits of life. So that is one thing, don't you think, my dear, good friends?'

Revenge

'As everyone knows,' he began, in his usual forceful, petulant manner, 'the universe belongs to the female of the species and the male – and this is not to the exclusion of man – is an accident of Creation.'

This statement, which came out of the blue, had annoyed me. I had just been telling him of my belief that what characterized the second half of the twentieth century was the emancipation of women, which I believed to be right and necessary after so many centuries of a slavery that was apparently accepted by them but that was, in fact, imposed by men.

He had appeared to be listening to me in agreement and approval and so his sudden interruption knocked me off course and the only thing that came to my mind was a pointless question.

'Do you think so?'

'Do I think so! I do, everyone does, even you, in spite of your ridiculous generosity, you will finally think so if you stop to consider the problem properly. You just have to study history, particularly small history, which can be proved more easily and is truer than the other, to come to this conclusion.'

We were sitting on the stone edge of the water tank, as Júlio the shoemaker, our hunting companion listened attentively. My long-standing friend, no one knew better than he the flights of partridges, nor their habits and behaviour in the region, and I could never consider a shoot without him. We had finished lunch after a fruitful morning and were now waiting in the shade for the sun, which in October still burns dreadfully, to cool its autumn heat a little. Five hundred metres away, almost vertically below us, the Douro was a strip of water, but in the afternoon all was so calm that we could hear its gentle gurgle, a distant promise of coolness.

After a short silence, Luís Claro, my guest and at times my rival, went on, 'For example, look at Napoleon. All his life that great general was ruled by women, and it was they who, to a large extent, determined his destiny.'

I made a sign of disagreement which I was unable to put into words.

'Don't you think so? Well just consider. During the time of the Directory he abandoned Italy, putting his victory at risk, in order to return to Paris, racing his horses, mad with jealousy for Josephine, who was drowning her sorrows in the arms of another man. Later, at the end of his life, he altered policy with the help of Maria Luisa of Austria, his legal wife, who twice deceived him with Metternich, the agent of the enemy. And so it goes on. Tell me, who led Anthony to his downfall? Wasn't it Cleopatra? And who ruled at the court of Charles the Great? Wasn't it his daughters and casual mistresses? And there's Attila, didn't he die in the arms of a woman? And Boabdil, didn't he sacrifice the kingdom of Grenada – the most beautiful of the Arab kingdoms – for the love of an adventuress in the pay of Isabella, *the Catholic*? Think about that woman who united Spain, of Catherine of Russia, of Christina of Sweden, and reflect that it all comes to down to them, be they perverted or virtuous, all in order to control men.

'I could give you thousands of examples, even without taking into account what's happening at the moment in our own country, in France, in England and, principally, in America. But there's no point, because were we to abandon history, which is always disputable and always hard to interpret, and descend to the hidden depths of biology, we should find instances far more easily and they would be far more convincing.

'I'm not talking about what happens between bees. In his *Life of the Bees*, when writing about the nuptial flight, Maeterlinck describes perfectly the death of the hero who takes the queen bee only to fall afterwards, its sexual organs removed, mortally wounded. I have seen how, after the impregnation of the queen, the female bees group together as the males enter the hive and gently hang from their wings in order to rip them off and leave them to die of starvation. I also have to remind you

101

that, while the praying mantis is being impregnated, she diverts herself by eating the head of the male. This example takes on a symbolic aspect because it is in effect by 'biting off his head' that woman manages to dominate man.'

I couldn't stop myself laughing and Júlio the shoemaker sketched a smile which encouraged me to bring him into the argument.

'And what about you, Júlio, you know more than anyone about insects and animals, so what do you think? Without meaning any disrespect to our friend Luís Claro, I think that on this matter your opinion is more valuable.'

Júlio the shoemaker blew his nose loudly on his large handkerchief and, flattered, started off, flattered.

'Well, Senhor Joãozinho, I have to say that I always find it hard to give my opinion. And I find it hard because giving an opinion on something you're not sure about is like handing out fake money. But as you want to hear it, here goes. I think that Senhor Luís Claro is partly right, but not entirely. I don't know anything about the famous men and women he talked about. And it's just as well I don't know, particularly things about the women.

'As for animals, that's another thing, as I've always lived with them. But that's where you've got to be really careful, because sometimes things happen the way Senhor Luís Claro says, and other times, lots of other times, the tables are turned. And as we are here shooting partridges, and doing well, I shall tell you about something I saw which I'll never forget even if I live to be a hundred. That and what happened afterwards, which is much more important.

In order to keep us on tenterhooks, knowing the curiosity he had excited, Júlio the shoemaker was silent for a moment and blew his nose loudly again.

'Well, once I was on Coucão hill, near Três Marias (Senhor Joãozinho knows it, but you don't, sir, as you aren't from around here), on a much steeper slope than this one, when from behind me I heard a rustle that I immediately thought must be a flock of partridges rising. I couldn't see them, and I wasn't in a position to shoot them, so I shaded my eyes in order to see whether I might work out where they were coming from and where they were going to, and then follow them. However, the rustle continued and when I turned round that's when I saw them, in the air and beyond reach. They were in total control and I can swear

102

to you that I'd never seen, and never saw again, so many partridges in one flock. There were more than thirty, and I immediately thought that they must be two flocks, which does happen sometimes at the start of a shoot, when the females haven't been shared out yet – something which would not be done peaceably.

'Estorninho, my dog, a sniffer dog, who was already old at the time and who hadn't noticed them, as the wind was in the opposite direction, had his head raised, just like me, following them with his eyes. They were flying high but I immediately realized in which direction they were going. "I'll eat my hat if they don't go and rest at the edge of Tresoiras, on the Mafarrico cliff."

'And just as I had thought, before turning the ridge, about a kilometre from where I stood, they descended like kites in a steep dive to land on a sort of gully there.

'That was when I made a decision that you certainly wouldn't agree with, knowing how well you still shoot these days, after twenty years. My thought was to catch them feeding on the ground and to see whether with a low shot, one of those that breaks their legs (not as easy as it may seem), I could wipe out half a dozen of them. I know that a shot in the air is far more beautiful and that it doesn't matter whether you get them with in the head, when they drop straight down, or you hit them in the stomach, when they fall half a league away, their legs stretched out, or even if you get them in the wing and go searching for them for two hours.

'Anyway, and you must forgive me for this, it seemed stupid to me to shoot into the air in order to kill just one, which even when you see it fall you don't know whether you're going to get to pick it up and put it on your belt, when you can take one shot on the ground and go and collect them as if you were picking up chestnuts.

'This what I immediately thought of, and without waiting I decided to warn Estorninho, who understood me just like you understand me, and I said to him, "Estorninho, today is a shoot in the old Portuguese style. You know what you've got to do." Estorninho had his pride as a dog and he wanted to find the birds and make them rise; he didn't like the idea of this travesty, but he also knew that on this matter I wasn't a man to be argued with. So when I began to walk he came behind me, as obedient and well-behaved as if he were a guard dog or a lady's lap dog, the kind that maids take for a walk in

103

the morning and at night to satisfy their needs.

'As for me, since these were young partridges I didn't know for sure whether they would hang on there or whether they would fly off again and, as it was getting late in the morning and the sun was beginning to burn, anything could happen. However, I couldn't let them rest for long and so I began to walk fast, almost run, as in those days I had legs that could carry me for many miles without getting tired, like a werewolf on a night of the full moon.

'In a flash I was a hundred metres from the place where I thought they had settled. Fortunately there was a high clump of bushes in front of the hide where I could conceal myself and so I began to advance slowly with the dog keeping close to my legs, making the least possible noise. I quickly reached the edge of the hide where, concealed behind a cluster of bushes, I knelt down and watched. At first I didn't see anything, and my thought was that they would be on the slope feeding in the rye field. This was, I imagined, what a partridge with any pride would do and it was, indeed, what they would have done had there not been for them, as there was at that moment, a far more important matter than filling their crop.

'In the middle of the dip was a large rock with a flat top which was about fifteen metres below me and perhaps twenty metres distant.

'It would never have entered my head that they would be there because partridges are not creatures who like to ruffle their feathers in open areas. But the fact is that they were there – they were all there and not one was missing. My heart skipped a beat and I began to prepare my gun and aim so that I could hit as many as possible. However, I didn't fire because what I saw was far more important to me than all the shoots in the world.

'The top of the rock was about ten metres by ten, but the partridges weren't together in a huddle like they often are, nor were they pecking at the grass or even idly nibbling as they always do. I could easily count them – there were exactly thirty-two. They were very quiet, with their necks stretched out, grouped in a circle, while in the middle two cock partridges were clucking in fury, their wings sweeping the ground, as they leapt, now advancing, now retreating, just like the fighting cocks in arenas in Braganza. All they lacked was iron spurs on their feet, but judging by their fury this was just as well for them.

'As for the hens, they looked like women sitting on the benches of a bullring watching the show. The only thing was that they weren't shouting, nor were they moving like I saw women doing in the Redondela bullring when I was once in Spain at an amazing fight. But that's another story that I'll tell you another day because although you might not think so, I, Júlio the shoemaker, am like the ship the *Catrineta*, and have many tales to tell, just as she did. But to go on.

'The difference between the ladies at the bullfight and the partridge ladies is that the bulls weren't fighting for the women, while the partridges knew very well that one of the cocks, if not the two, would die for love of them. And there they were, highly satisfied with life, as though this tribute was due to them and that the males of this world were created for nothing other than to fight for them. And now, at this point, I must explain to you, Senhor Claro, why in the world of hen partridges everything is as though the cocks were born for nothing other than their pleasure and satisfaction.

'The fact is that hen partridges are like chickens, the difference being that chickens lay all year round, while partridges only lay once, or at most twice if the weather, animals or men damage the first nest. Even so, they need to be impregnated all year round, even when it isn't the time for fertilisation and breeding, because a partridge who doesn't have a cock to flap its wings over her for her enjoyment loses her chirp and her appetite, just like a young girl whose fiancé has been stolen from her or has died on the eve of her wedding.

'But not all of them are there for that – only the strongest – because on this the hens are most demanding. For that reason we see those flocks of suitors comprising only males, who are nothing more than frustrated birds who have managed to prove far less to the hens than any of us.

'And for sure the hens don't hang from their wings like bees do, but they do put them to flight from their favourite feeding grounds, which are always the best. For that reason the cocks are thin and as tough as horn.

'Anyway, I stayed there with my gun in my hand, my eyes fixed on them and not concerned about whether I should hide, as I knew that none of them, hens or cocks, was paying attention to me. So then, after the dance, which was just the beginning, the cocks began to wrestle, pecking at each other as much as they could, with feathers flying everywhere. This lasted five minutes, if that, until one of them gave the final thrust to the other. It all happened in a second and suddenly I saw the conqueror with his feet on top of the other, crowing with satisfaction, as though he wanted to throw the echo of his victory to the mountain slopes. The hens remained stock still as though awaiting orders, and when the cock tired of crowing and flew off they all followed him, without turning their heads to look at the misery of the one that was dying for sake of them.

'You know, Senhor Claro, and Senhor Joãozinho knows even better, that I've killed hundreds, if not thousands, of partridges and that I've never hesitated in hitting their heads with a stone when they fall or are badly injured and are still in their death throes. But although it hurts me to say it, I have to confess that the agony of that creature affected me as though it were the agony of a human. When I went down to it, it was to give it a merciful blow, not to take it home and eat it. I wanted to finish it off and bury it, almost, God forgive me, wanting to give it a Christian burial as one would for a creature with a soul.

'But I didn't even have the courage for that, for if it's the soul that gives one the strength to live or die, then that creature had the soul of the strongest.

'The ground was covered with drops of blood and feathers, but no sooner had I got to the top of the rock – and it wasn't very easy – the partridge stood up, shaking on its legs as though it wanted to stand on guard and fight another enemy.

'It was then that I thought of taking it home and looking after it, so that I could then set it free once it could stand properly on its legs. No sooner said than done. I caught it with my hat and then put it under my shirt, next to my chest, which is the best way of carrying an injured bird.

'When I got home I paid no attention to what my wife was saying, nor to the squeals of my children, but began to examine the creature properly so that I might treat it as best I could. The partridge had a broken wing and a deep wound on its neck and it seemed certain that it wouldn't survive. But I decided, whatever the case to try, and with soft mud (which is what partridges do themselves), I made a cast to straighten the wing, and after washing the wound I sewed it neatly with a binding needle. It was only after this that I went to eat, leaving the future in God's hands. And what happened was that, after four days, Pimpão – that's the name I gave it – was drinking water, eating corn and even grit, which partridges swallow to fill their crop as ballast to help them to fly.

' "This is a real man," I thought, still having the idea of setting it free so that it could follow its destiny.

'But it's one thing to make a decision and another to act on it... And this is where the real story begins.'

Júlio the shoemaker was silent, wanting to gauge the effect of his story and keep us on edge. The sun was by now rising above the Meadas mountain range and one of those calm autumn afternoons on the Douro was beginning to open the fading petals of its golden corolla.

Then, suddenly, he suggested, 'What about going and taking some more shots?'

' "No, Júlio,' I replied hastily – "I'm not taking another shot and I'm not killing another partridge, without hearing the rest of the story."

' "Nor me," Luís Claro agreed.

' "Well, if that's how you want it, here we go."

Then, after clearing his throat and coughing in order to fine-tune his voice, he went on.

'The days went by and two weeks later, early in the morning, I woke to hear the loud sound of him crowing. He was singing away, like a cock partridge who knows perfectly what he has to do.

'I had made him a cage, but most of the time he would walk freely in the kitchen, pecking away here and foraging there, perfectly happy with the dog and the cat, to whom I had laid down the law. And I should tell you that I always talked to the animals and they always understood me. So when I got hold of them, I told them straight what I was thinking, "Friend Estorninho and friend Liró, Pimpão is a member of the household, like you, and you don't touch him. I want peace and quiet and you are all to get on." And what I said held. Liró stopped bristling and Estorninho stopped giving him a sideways look as though waiting to pounce. In the end he would perch on Estorninho's back and gently peck at him as though picking at fleas.

'I was happy that morning when I heard him sing, but then I was sad. I'm not a man who breaks a promise, not even if I make it to myself; the time had come to set him free.'

'At lunch I told my wife and children of my decision and there was a chorus of protest. "Oh, listen, think what harm you're doing to the creature! Let him stay," my wife protested. "Oh, daddy, don't do that," my children begged. "I must," I argued. "I promised that I would let him go and that's what I've got to do."

'After lunch we all went to the bottom of the garden where the slope starts – it's a good place for a bird who's not used to flying. It hurt me too, but my word is my bond and has to be kept, even though it was all to do with an animal. My hand was shaking when I took the bird out of the cage, put it on the top of the wall and talked to it, saying, "Pimpão, the time has come. Go and see if you can find your enemy and steal the hens from him. God works in strange ways."

'The bird had turned its head towards me and was staring at me, as though understanding, but it didn't move.

' "Come on," I told it, "you've got a straight wing and your crop is full of stones. Come on."

'And since he wouldn't make up his mind, and so as not to prolong the scene that was tearing at our hearts, I picked him up and tossed him into the air. The bird flapped its wings until it adjusted its flight and then off it went, as though knowing exactly where it wanted to go. We stood there watching it, and then to our surprise we suddenly saw it turn like a homing pigeon and fly towards us, landing exactly on the spot where I had put it. Impatiently I got hold of him and put him in the cage.

' "God has His reasons, and this creature knows perfectly well what it wants to do." And with relieved hearts we went back into the house.

'The partridge was singing so much, morning and evening, that even in Meijão-Frio, which is two kilometres away, everyone knew that I, Júlio the shoemaker, had a partridge in the house. I wasn't happy about this because, as everyone knows, it's against the law to keep partridges in cages and there would surely be someone who, through jealousy, would go and report me at the barracks. The reason I thought this was because of the old saying that, "from Meijão-Frio to Baião, neither a man nor a dog, neither wind nor a wedding", which frankly, between us, is hardly ever true, because both Senhor Joãozinho and I live in the district and no one can say we have done anything harmful to anyone.

'What was for sure was that the bird would sing and I couldn't and wouldn't tell it to keep quiet. But as I know very well who I'm dealing with, I started to work on what I was going to say when Commander Antunes – whom God now has in His protection and who was never a bad person, but who also wasn't a particularly good person – would bring up the subject in a roundabout way, as was his custom. So as I had predicted, one fine morning he turned up at the shop saying that he needed his shoes repaired and that I was to stretch some boots that were tight on him; and then he fired at me, "It's the end of the shooting season and you, Senhor Júlio, haven't paid me my share."

'I used to give him two partridges, and it is true that that year I hadn't yet given them to him. However, as I was prepared for this I used this cue to raise the matter.

' "You're right, Commander Antunes, but this year I just didn't want to shoot and didn't even pick up my gun. I really don't know whether I'll ever pick it up again or whether I'll leave it to rust on the hook above the chest."

' "Don't tell me!" he retorted. "The best huntsman in the region (these were his words, not mine), crafty as a setter, not going to shoot any more. No, I don't believe it. What made this happen? Did you hit someone?"

"You're way off the mark, Commander Antunes, I didn't hit any-one, but something happened to me that shook me up inside, something that you'd only believe if you saw it."

'Looking directly at him I told him the whole story about my par-tridge, much embellished, as even a commander, however nasty his soul is, is capable of being moved. And as soon as I got to the part where I let it free and it flew back to the same place... I saw that he had enjoyed the story and I stopped talking, waiting, as I had worked out quite well what he was going to say. And so it was.

' "Senhor Júlio, that's an amazing story, but the fact is that you cannot have a partridge in a cage because the law doesn't allow it. I don't know what we can do about it."

' "Nor me, Commander Antunes, sir..." And here I added the 'sir' in order to soften him. "Nor me. That's why I had already made up my mind to come and see you, to ask your advice, as the fact is that I don't know what I should do. Kill it? No. Set it free? It doesn't want that. The only thing to do is to give it – but then we'd be in the same boat. Anyway, if you want it... I'd give it to you with pleasure, Commander Antunes."

' "To me? I hardly want it in the barracks."

'I wasn't hoping to get out of this easily and took advantage of his silence to ask artfully, "Does the law state absolutely that you can't keep partridges in a cage?"

' "No, it's not exactly that. It says that you can't keep partridges captive in the house."

' "Ah! Then Commander Antunes, we're OK, because I don't keep it in the house. I've got it in the hen house, with the other birds."

' "This was a lie, but when a lie is for the good of someone then it's the work of God, and men do wrong to disbelieve it."

' "Right," said Commander Antunes, who wanted to give in. "That changes everything. Is your hen house more than twenty metres from the house?"

' "More than fifty. It's at the end of the orchard."

' "Well then," he went on, "if that's the case – and because that's what you're telling me – it can't be seen as an outbuilding. Perhaps the law is being sophistic (he had learnt this grand word when sitting in on trials), but others, even judges, have done that and no one has charged them. You are lucky, and so is your partridge, because I'm going to shut my eyes to it. The more so because I know that you aren't one to use bait when hunting.

' "Me use bait? That's something I've never done." (This was true, I had never done that.)

' "I know. But there's one condition. I'm not letting you off my share and the sooner the better. And remember that there are nine of us in the barracks needing to eat."

' "Don't worry, you won't be lacking partridges."

'Commander Antunes left and I was happy as a lark. So happy that I began to sing my favourite song.

Shoemaker, hammer the sole
Ai, cataboom, cataboom!
For hammering is a comfort
Ai, cataboom, cataboom!

'I went back to the house and told the family what had happened. I was so delighted that I even let my sons have a second glass. When I went to bed – and this wasn't usual for me – I couldn't walk straight, my legs were so wobbly. It was only the next day – I swear to this – that I thought about what Commander Antunes had said to me. "You're not a man to hunt with bait." These words never left my thoughts. For a week I churned it over and one night, when I was in bed, I gave a shout that even my wife woke up in fright.

' "So why shouldn't I hunt with bait?" '

' "What? What are you saying?" '

' "Nothing. Set the alarm for four; I'm going hunting in the morning – a long way from here." '

'The next day was a Sunday and my wife muttered, "What about Mass?"

' "Don't worry, I'll go to the one o'clock service tomorrow like the *fidalgos*." '

'I didn't need the alarm to go off, as at three thirty I was up. I had a coffee, filled my cartridge belt, wrapped Pimpão's cage in an old blanket and off I went with my gun over my shoulder, walking fearlessly to the Provinco hills, which are about a league from anywhere that's inhabited. I was thinking, quite rightly, that I'd be very unlucky if anyone – most of all the men at the barracks, who like to be at the ready – should come across me, since I was taking such care.

'Once I'd reached the spot I hid the cage in a gorse bush and prepared a hiding place for myself in a clump of broom. I made a seat with a stone so that I could sit and wait in comfort. But I didn't need to wait long. Just as the day dawned, Pimpão was singing, tuning his voice like someone who is aware of the task he had been set. And I was quite sure that the partridge wouldn't restrain himself. In fact it didn't take long for them to reply, lots of them from all sides, and I saw straight away that there was a never-ending supply of them. Ten minutes hadn't gone by and I'd already killed three. My concern was that the partridge would fall silent if it was frightened by the shots. But no. The more partridges I killed the more the partridge sang, and I could swear that it wasn't to call them but rather in anger and satisfaction.

'An hour later I had already got nine partridges – the same number as the commander and soldiers. "That's enough for today," I thought, picked up my bag and made my way straight back home.

'When she saw me with so many birds my wife's eyes bulged with excitement.

' "Lord, so many!" '

' "Yes, there are a lot, but they're not for us. They're for Commander Antunes, because they're his by right." '

'It was a form of compensation for the deception I'd committed, and it still wasn't eleven when there I was at the door of the barracks with that fantastic bag.

' "The word of a shoemaker is no less than that of a king. What was promised was a debt. Here you are."

' "Good God, man, how did you do that?" he asked, clearly distrustful.

' "Surely you know, Commander Antunes, that one day is good for the hunted and the next is good for the hunter. Today was my day."

'For more than a week I was pondering over what I had done and suddenly an idea came to me that wouldn't let me rest. There were three days until the end of the season and so I had no chance to wait for Sunday. It was a Tuesday, I remember it well, and at dinner I said to my wife, "Tomorrow morning I'm not going to work, I'm going shooting. You can go to the shop and tell the apprentices that I've gone to Régua to buy materials."

'My wife wasn't one of those who ask why, and without adding more, she simply said, "Fine."

' "And keep your mouth shut, OK?"

' "Don't worry, I shall."

'This time I didn't need the alarm clock, as I couldn't sleep. It was still night when I was at the chosen place with Pimpão – the place where I had watched the battle between the two partridges. My idea was to see what he would do when he realized where he was.

'It was still hardly light but he began to sing, and immediately the hens started to reply. I didn't see them, but I could hear the flutter of their wings. The sound of the hens is a graceful gurgle, and I knew that it was females who were responding. But suddenly another sound arose – as strong as my partridge's, the song of a cock, driving off any company and not wanting competition.

'From where it was it could see the cage and so could see that Pimpão's feathers were ruffled and his neck stretched out. With the leaps he was making the cage was shaking so much that I feared it would roll down the slope. Then he began a battle song that didn't stop, in which there was so much fury that I trembled.

'I pointed my gun, because I knew very well what was going to happen. And I didn't have to wait long. With his wings tucked in, the other partridge descended in a dive towards the cage. I carefully took aim and when it was about ten metres away I fired. It fell down flat, like a stick, and almost landed on top of the cage.

'As for me, there was no doubt. The partridge was the one that had injured Pimpão. I had no doubt, and nor did he. You just had to see the anger with which he was pecking at the bars.

'Then the idea came to me to see what would happen if I let him loose, and without hesitating I opened the door.

'With his wings dragging on the ground, Pimpão walked slowly towards the dead bird and suddenly jumped on it and began pecking at it. He quickly realized that it was pointless. With a short flight he perched on top of the rock and began to crow again. The hens started to come to the call and he had a good dozen and a half round him.

'The partridge fell silent and there in front of me began to impregnate them, as though he had kept his year-long fertility just for that moment. I'm convinced that he was doing it to ensure their submission, and they certainly snuggled up with no resistance.

'I felt satisfied, as though this was happening to me – satisfied as though I were watching an act of justice. I knew that I was going to lose a friend, but I had helped to prepare his revenge. I had no regrets.

'Pimpão gave a loud crow and with a noisy beat of his wings took flight, followed by the flock.'

Júlio the shoemaker fell silent and then, with a smile, remarked, 'As you can see, Senhor Luís Claro, sometimes the tables are turned.' And he went on, 'And it pleases God that for the good of us all (us men and the women) this will continue until the end of the world.'

Publications
of the Center for Portuguese Studies

Studies on Jorge de Sena by His Colleagues and Friends, ed.
Harvey L. Sharrer and Frederick G. Williams

Camoniana Californiana, ed. Maria de Lourdes Belchior
Pontes and Enrique Martinez-Lopez

Carlos Drummond de Andrade and His Generation, ed. Frederick
G. Williams and Sérgio Pachá

*In the Beginning There Was Jorge de Sena's GENESIS: The Birth
of a Writer*, Francisco Cota Fagundes

The Evidences (bilingual), Jorge de Sena, trans. Phyllis
Sterling Smith

The Portuguese and the Pacific I, ed. Francis A. Dutra and João
Camilo dos Santos

O Amor das Letras e das Gentes, ed. João Camilo dos Santos
and Frederick G. Williams

Camilo Castelo Branco, No Centenário da Morte, ed. João Camilo
dos Santos

The Baron, Branquinho da Fonseca, ed. and trans. Francisco
Cota Fagundes

Three Short Stories by Eça de Queirós, ed. João Camilo dos
Santos, trans. Christopher Lund

Initiation into Portuguese Literature, António José Saraiva; eds.
João Camilo dos Santos and Marcelo Moreschi;
trans. Christopher Lund

Singular People, Manuel Teixeira Gomes, ed. João Camilo
dos Santos, trans. Christopher Lund

Santa Barbara Portuguese Studies, I–XI